The Night Riders Mystery

The Night Riders Mystery

Martina Eberhard

Copyright: © 2010 Martina Eberhard
Original title: Fånga tjuvryttarna!
Cover photos: girl © Bob Langrish, horse © Marielle Andersson Gueye
Cover layout: Stabenfeldt A/S

Translated by Kjell Johansson
Typeset by Roberta L. Melzl
Editor: Bobbie Chase
Printed in Germany, 2010

ISBN: 978-1-934983-62-1

Stabenfeldt, Inc.
225 Park Avenue South
New York, NY 10003
www.pony.us

Available exclusively through PONY.

Chapter One

Maddie and I were sitting on the bench outside the stable. The stable roof had just enough overhang that we didn't get wet from the endless, steadily falling June rain. I could see Coolie out in the paddock, the rain turning her dark brown coat almost black as rivulets of water ran over her fetlock and tail.

"It's been raining for three days!" Maddie complained, sighing hopelessly. She held her bare foot out, feeling the drops.

"We could win our swimming badges in the riding paddock," I grumped, making the little hole in my black T-shirt bigger by pressing my index finger through it. The hole was a dear memory of the litter of puppies that my mom had raised this spring. They managed to bite holes in most of my clothes. They've all moved away to their new homes, and I still get tears in my eyes when I think about Clown, the last puppy we sold. But then, of course, I still have my own dog Sis; my beautiful Irish setter girl who's full of mischief and sweetness.

"Three days of rain and three days of summer vacation – what a coincidence! And last week when we were still in school, the heat was almost tropical," Maddie complained, waving her bare toes in the rain. Her toes, like the rest of her, were a warm golden brown – Maddie was adopted from Colombia, South America, and moved here to Sweden. My own feet were more a shade called Nordic pig pink.

I watched Coolie, who was methodically grazing out in the pasture. As usual, I was filled with a warm joy when I realized that I actually owned my very own horse. She's been my very own horse for five months now, and sometimes I almost have to pinch myself to remember that she isn't just an unusually real dream. All my life, for as long as I can remember, I dreamed of owning a horse. I used to draw dream horses and make up names and pedigrees for them, and then play that all of it was real. Back when I lived in Uppsala (here in Sweden) my best friend Linda and I used to gallop around the driveway, playing horses. We were the most well trained ten-year-olds in the world, since we "rode" for hours every day and carried on lots of advanced jumping competitions at full gallop.

At that time, back when I was around ten, I fantasized a lot about a snow-white Arabian stallion that I would name Silver Dream, or an all-black Friesian horse with a mane reaching down to his knees.

Coolie is neither a snow-white Arabian nor a black Friesian. She's an ordinary dark brown half-blood mare with a black mane and tail and a star on her forehead. She has a slightly deformed back, since her withers are disproportionately big, making her look sway-backed and older than her eight years. Her lower lip hangs down a little, giving her a somewhat grumpy face. But her eyes are as lovely as you can imagine, she's long-legged and her Thoroughbred-like body is elegant, and when you get her into a collected gallop and she really goes for it, she is just beautiful.

I love my horse, sway-backed or not, and I've decided to not listen to stuck-up horse-girls who say nasty things about Coolie behind our backs, calling her "the camel" or "the hammock." Comments like those used to make my heart ache, but I'm not listening to them any more.

Coolie suddenly lifted her head up from the grass and pricked her ears in our direction.

"Hello, my little sugar!" I called out, waving at her.

I couldn't hear her neighing in the rain, but I could see from the ripples on her chest that she answered me with a singing neigh before she returned to the juicy grass again. This was another endearing aspect of Coolie's personality: she answered when you spoke to her, and as soon as I came into the yard she recognized my footsteps and said hello by neighing loudly. How lovely is that?

"Sugar! Well, you're going to make me blush," I heard Vibeke's voice below our dangling legs.

Maddie laughed and knowingly poked me with her elbow. "Sucking up to the boss, eh?"

I blushed, as usual, and felt silly. Maddie knew that I embarrassed easily and would often tease me, but never in a mean way – Maddie is one of the nicest people I've ever met and I was glad to find a really good friend after we moved to Skåne, in the far south of Sweden, a year ago.

"I thought we'd take the horses in to de-worm them, and Jörgen has Isa now so this seems like a good time." Vibeke, my neighbor and the owner of the farm where I keep Coolie, is an accomplished dressage rider and breeder of half-breed horses. I had worked for her all fall and winter, when she was expecting baby Isa and needed help with all the horses on her farm. Now there are three mares, one of which recently foaled. Besides those four beautiful girls, there's also a two-year-old prankster named Spotlight who wreaks havoc at the farm, eagerly egged on by his stable mate, a gelding named Tartan.

"We're coming!" Maddie said, starting to climb down the wooden ladder that was leaning against the bale of silage.

We started with Disa and her filly Mona. Maddie and I totally love Disa's beautiful little baby. She's a wonder of long, gracious legs, little cute doll's feet and fawn-like eyes with sweeping, light brown lashes. Everything about her is just so small and cuddly. Her muzzle is finely shaped and soft as velvet – well, you really could eat her up with a spoon, that's how cute she is! Her short curled stump of a tail whipped about as she danced around her mom in happy little prances.

Disa obediently followed us into her box with Mona dancing around her. Mona still kept close to her mom and always seemed a little worried that we would take her mother away from her when we took Disa into the paddock or out of it. The time had come for Mona's first de-worming, and I was a little tense about it, as I'd never de-wormed a foal before.

The next pair in was Coolie and Cissi. They looked like siblings as they walked; big and dark brown, and each with a star on her forehead. Coolie went one step behind me at all times, pushing her muzzle against the

9

small of my back. I've never been able to understand why she does this, but it's so cuddly. Amaryllis, the beautiful dressage diva of the stable, sounded insulted as she neighed from the paddock. How could we leave her for last?

"It'll be your turn in a while, just take it easy!" I yelled at her before we went clattering onto the concrete floor of the stable. Soon all the horses were stabled and all of them were expectantly looking out from their boxes, probably thinking they were going to get concentrated feed, having no idea they were in for some not quite so delicious de-worming paste. My left hip still hurt from Spotlight tackling me into the water trough with an impressive push. That rascal was responsible for lots of my bruises, tender toes and swollen lips. He was lucky to be so beautiful and sweet, because it's probably saved him from the slaughterer's van every time.

And now it was time for Circus De-Worming to begin. Cissi obediently swallowed her dose, dear old Cissi. Amaryllis threw her head up and down a little but then finally settled down. Coolie probably thought this was some new way of being fed and almost slurped the paste, and then she got this look on her face, as if she were a little fooled and a little disappointed in me, which got us laughing. Tartan needed some persuasion, but Vibeke's commanding voice and sure hands calmed him down.

Spotlight, however, as expected, challenged everybody's patience. Finally, Vibeke put one hand over his eyes and grabbed his tongue with the other, and quick as a flash Maddie was there with the syringe, pushing the paste into his mouth. Spotlight smacked his lips and grimaced for ten minutes, to the delight of his audience.

The challenge of the day was no doubt the mother and daughter in the spacious foal box. Disa swallowed obediently, but little Mona didn't want the nasty plastic syringe in her mouth. She reared and swung around in the box, her tail whipping angrily. Disa didn't like us forcing her foal and laid her ears back before aiming a forceful kick at the box wall with her hind legs. I jumped away in terror as Vibeke put a calming hand on Disa's back.

"Well now, girl, easy now, we won't hurt her," she cooed to Disa, who was still blowing through her dilated nostrils excitedly and keeping her ears back as a warning. I felt respect for her motherly wrath and didn't want to be hit by those hind legs, which she kept lifting to hold us back. Maddie calmly stayed in the box – she never seemed afraid of horses, which made me feel like a real wimp.

Maddie was raised in a trotting stable and she still helped her dad with all the horses there. In the beginning, I had been pretty skeptical about Maddie coming to Vibeke's stable, but Maddie was so confident and relaxed with the horses, and seemed to be a natural when it came to riding. I guess I'll have to admit that I was simply jealous, and afraid that she would take over my rightful place in Vibeke's stable. Instead, we actually got to be really good friends. Maddie is great, a real trustworthy buddy. Also, I soon realized that having my own horse took up a lot of my time, and I didn't have close to the same amount of time for Vibeke's horses anymore. I never thought I'd say it, but it was actually nice not to have to ride Vibeke's horses anymore, now that her doctor had allowed her to start riding again. Coolie needed a lot of time, and I had promised myself to be a better master to Sis, my lovely Irish setter, whom I had been neglecting a little for the last year.

"Grab my fleece over there, Anna!" Vibeke pointed to a dark brown fleece jacket hanging over the box door. "Put it around Disa's head and tie the sleeves together." I had to stand on my toes to reach Disa's head, and it was only with some effort that I could knot the sleeves under her cheeks.

"Now just hold Disa, Anna, and let's see if we can get the de-worming paste into this little rascal!" Vibeke grabbed the foal's halter and Maddie held her arms around the lanky little body. Mona kicked her legs and bucked in protest, but Maddie and Vibeke held her tightly and calmly and finally managed to give her the required dose. Disa objected a little, neighing to her foal, but I managed to hold her without being kicked or bitten.

"Operation De-Worming successfully completed!" Vibeke said with satisfaction, and then we laughed at how we looked: tousled, sweaty and totally dirty from the de-worming paste, mixed with grass-green froth from the horses – nice.

Maddie and I decided to brave the rain and go riding. Our horses had been grazing outside for three days now without being ridden. Coolie was getting a grass stomach, and I had decided not to allow her to swell into that pregnant-in-the-tenth-month look that was brought on by too much nutritious grass and lack of exercise. I'd already had to widen the saddle girth by one hole, even though summer vacation had just begun.

We tied our horses in the passageway and started grooming. Maddie was riding Amaryllis, as her own Thoroughbred, Hot Shot, was grazing at home at their farm. The horses seemed to have been washed by the rain, so we didn't have to groom them much before they shone and sparkled. I took the opportunity to spray some coat shine on Coolie's mane and tail and fix a few tail knots with a plastic curry comb. The good thing about the rain was that the horses weren't bothered by flies and mosquitoes. Coolie's new top-of-the-line fly-mask was lying unused in the stable box.

Water splashed and sprinkled around our horses' hooves as we clattered along the gravel road that led to the woods. Luckily, we'd managed to hit a short break from the rain, and we crossed our fingers hoping that this would last for our entire ride. The horses seemed to like this interruption in their three-day-long eating binge and walked easily, their heads weaving in different directions to study the well-known surroundings. Coolie jumped aside for a mailbox that she'd passed fifty times before, and suddenly Amaryllis started trotting while she was walking on long reins, just like little kids with lots of energy.

"So, you're going for it today!" I said, patting Coolie's shoulder. She answered by snorting and shaking her head. You feel quite statuesque when you're rocking around on a horse that's almost six feet tall. Most horses seemed small compared to Coolie – Vibeke had a few really large horses, although Amaryllis was just fifteen hands high, which meant that I could look down at Maddie. They were a beautiful package, Maddie and Amaryllis. Amaryllis was a golden chestnut with a nice straight blaze and two white half-stockings on her forelegs. She was Vibeke's competition horse and performed difficult dressage. You could see that she was an accomplished competition horse; she moved with such grace and energy. It was really hard to sit down on her when she was trotting; you'd get thrown around like a beginner. Vibeke explained that that's how it was with really good dressage horses; they were hard to sit on at a trot and needed a special technique with your hips to make everything look easy and elegant. It seemed that Maddie, unlike me, had been born with that technique – she had a great ability to mount any horse and just become one with it. To me, it always felt unusual and backwards to get up on a new horse, and I always had to struggle for a while before I became sure of what I was sitting on. By now, I was used to large horses, but my first weeks with Coolie had been dizzying and scary. She took such great big steps that I felt like a beginner again when I bounced around on top of her. At first she seemed a little too big for me, since I'm kind of skinny and not very tall, but I soon realized that technique, not strength, was what was needed to make Coolie collect herself and walk in correct form.

We turned onto the woodland road and the horses started jig-jogging in expectation. Their hooves squelched on the rain-dampened ground. The misty summer air was heavily scented with moss and fir needles. I felt a tingling happiness in my stomach. Here I was on my own horse, a damp and soft woodland road wound invitingly in front of us, the summer vacation had just begun, and I had finally gotten through nine long years of school.

"Want to trot? A little warm-up before the gallop stretch." Maddie collected her reins and urged Amaryllis on, and the horse quickly answered by going off at a trot. Coolie followed her with great strides. She didn't like to be second, probably due to her father's galloping genes.

"Easy now, girl. We'll pass them, as soon as we start galloping," I said to Coolie, whose ears were pricked toward Amaryllis's bouncing hindquarters. I had to rein Coolie in quite a lot to keep her behind Maddie and Amaryllis. After a couple of miles we reached the desired straightaway, slightly sloping upwards. I just needed to put my left leg a couple of inches forward, and Coolie was galloping. I stood up in a hunt seat and grabbed hold of her mane with my left hand while my right hand shortened the reins, so as not to lose control. My eyes filled with tears from the wind, and the tears promptly were blown backwards toward my ears before the wind blew them off altogether. Then my nose started running – I could never understand why my nose always started to run when I was riding. Amaryllis's hooves threw up mud and rainwater that hit both Coolie and me. The speed made my stomach tingle even more, and the pounding hooves made me want to ride even faster. It was wonderful and a little scary at the same time, but mostly wonderful! Soon Coolie's head was even with Maddie's legs. Coolie kept going like a real race horse, pressing forward to pass them. The woodland road was our racetrack and the strip of grass in the middle separated our different tracks. Maddie threw us a glance and seemed to ease her hand a little when she saw that we were passing, but Coolie was an unbelievable sprinter when it came to galloping, and her long legs stretched like a panther's when she thundered along like a fast train through the woods. Metal clinked against metal as Maddie's and my stirrups struck each other when we were side by side. My reins were still short and I was still urging Coolie on, but now I let my hand move three inches forward and huddled under the wind that was pulling at my clothes. The speed exhilarated me, and my body felt a mixture of fear and happiness. Hooves pounded and Coolie snorted with excitement when she took the lead. I blinked wildly so I could see, and suddenly realized that the right turn by the pond was coming up at rocket speed and that I didn't have that much road left to slow down. My heart hammered in my chest and I desperately grabbed the reins to slow Coolie down. I leaned back in the saddle as heavily as I could and practically held my right hand behind my own hip. What would happen if I couldn't stop her? The turn was sharp and tree-lined, and we'd probably fall over in the turn and almost kill ourselves. And then my mom wouldn't let me ride ever again! Coolie threw her head back and forth, protesting over my rough handling of the reins.

"Ssssslow down, ssslow, Coolie!" I urged in a shaky voice. Suddenly, our speed seemed dangerous and not at all beautiful anymore. I regretted urging Coolie on and steaming past Maddie. The curve was only fifty feet ahead of us and it pained me to tear so roughly at Coolie's sensitive mouth, but I was desperate so pulled for all I was worth, really sawing at her mouth, and just a few feet before the sharp turn I managed to get her down to a slow canter, almost at a standstill, before I finally stopped her altogether. I leaned toward her mane and breathed deeply, wiping my tear-filled eyes and dripping nose with the sleeve of my sweater. My heart beat so hard that I could hear it echoing against my ribs. Coolie turned around and was ready to get going again when Amaryllis came galloping and stopped nicely and gently in front of us. I was glad that there hadn't been a witness to my disastrous stop.

"Oh wow! What a speed freak you are!" Maddie shook her head and laughed.

"I totally forgot about the turn by the pond! And then I couldn't see anything because my eyes were tearing and Coolie just went crazy. I could barely stop her! I thought we'd crash right out into the trees and kill ourselves!"

"Well, you can sure see that her dad was a galloping champion! I can hardly believe how she went for it."

Maddie seemed impressed, while I was still mostly relieved that we weren't lying in a big heap of broken bones among the spruces.

We let our horses cool down by jogging easily on long reins. Vibeke had taught us how important it was to cool down and get the lactic acid out of the horses' muscles to avoid aches later.

As we walked on the gravel road, we could feel raindrops starting to fall. A wind was blowing, which made the rain fall almost horizontally and whip our faces. I lowered my head and pulled my helmet a little lower down on my forehead to avoid getting rain in my eyes.

"Lousy weather!" I complained, shuddering from the cold. My wet sweater clung to my body like an icy bandage. Swedish summers …

"Well, we had a little while there without rain anyway," my unbearably positive friend countered. Maddie seldom complained about things, and she had an unusual ability to see the best in things and people. She made me feel like a bad person when we were watching Idol or some other TV show and I discovered how often I commented on somebody's ugly hairdo or weird dialect, while Maddie always kept defending them with, "but still, she has a pretty face," or, "I think that actually sounds nice." I was trying to become a better person and not complain all the time.

We decided that our horses would get to stand inside after our riding session, to warm up a little in their dry, cozy boxes. I took the pad from my saddle and hung it on the heater in the tack room. Vibeke had a washing machine in the stable, but it felt a little greedy to borrow hers when we had one at home. Mom had forbidden me to wash and dry horse things. She had had to call a repairman who had to clean the washer and the drain after I'd washed sweat blankets and saddle pads. Six hundred Swedish crowns, which is over eighty dollars – expensive!

Speaking of expensive, at dinner that night Mom told me it cost too much money for me to go to riding camp when I had my own horse. I tried to explain how important it was to grow as a rider and to learn from different trainers.

"But Anna, how do you suppose you're going to pay for that?" Mom's eyes bored into me. The determined Economy-Mom was in full force, the mom who always talked about how much apples cost while I was filling my pockets with fruit for Coolie. And the mom who had some voodoo sixth sense ability to know how much the farrier, vaccinations and de-worming had cost during the last month. I personally had no idea and was always flabbergasted when Mom cited outrageous sums. It really was expensive to keep a horse, much more expensive than I'd ever imagined before we got Coolie.

My best defense was that it actually had been Mom's idea to get me a horse. It was a kind of bribe to make me to agree to move down to Skåne, away from my beloved borrowed horse Sesame and my best friend Linda, to where Mom had gotten a great job at an advertising agency.

"But I'll be working in Vibeke's stable for a month and Dad's going to send us money. It always works out in the end, you know." I stared back at her as I drank some cold milk. Kalle and Jonatan, my shameless four-year-old twin brothers, made rude noises with a bottle of ketchup and laughed wildly.

"Can you stop doing that!" I hissed, jerking the bottle of ketchup away from them.

"Give here! Anna stinks!" Jonatan tried to reach the bottle and overturned his full glass of milk, making Mom jump out of her chair.

"Can't you just sit down and eat in peace even one single time!" my mother yelled, marching away for some kitchen towels. At least she forgot about our economic dilemma for a while. I quickly sneaked away from the kitchen table and locked the door to my room to prevent potential twin invasion.

A while later I was on the Internet, enjoying the muffled pings that meant that somebody was sending me a message. Linda was often online, Maddie once in while, and Dad could be online every now and then. Right now a few horse girls that I'd gotten to know in Skåne were chatting on MSN.

"Are you coming to Uppsala this summer?" Linda asked.

"I'll be working at Vibeke's for four weeks, then one week taking care of trotters at Maddie's and another week dressage camp at Omset riding school. Then I WAAANT to go to Uppsala!"

"Feels like it's been 500 years since I saw you!"

"I know, miss you and all a lot! :-o"

"You're my BFF! Have to go now. Angelica and I are going to the Fyris pool. Hugs & kisses."

I sighed deeply, missing the Fyris pool – it felt like ages since Linda and I had spent our summer afternoons at the pool. Often, we'd spend the morning at the stable, taking care of our beloved keeping horses, Mackan and Sesame, and then we'd cool off at the outdoor pool in town. I remember how we'd eat popsicles until our tongues screamed in garish colors, and how we'd urge each other to jump from the 30-foot tower. I could feel the smell of chlorine and the thrill of falling 30 feet straight down and hitting the water before you tumbled around in slow motion under the surface and started floundering to get back to the surface.

This felt like memories from long ago, and although I

22

always wrote to Linda that we'd be best friends forever and that I missed her terribly, I had begun to suspect that this was getting less and less true. Linda mostly felt like old memories and my feelings for her were fading like old photographs. Sometimes I ached with guilt when I felt this, but then I also suspected that the same thing was happening to her. Out of some kind of duty we wrote that we were going to see each other, and maybe we wanted this a little, but then we were almost relieved when something came up to stop our reunion.

I decided to go to bed early, so I turned my computer off and went out to brush my teeth. The twins were curled up in the sofa, watching some cartoon, while Mom was doing something on her laptop.

"Are you going to bed already?" Mom said in surprise when she saw me in my checkered pajama pants and top.

"I'll be going to Vibeke's at seven tomorrow so I thought I might as well."

"I can wake you up if you want. Some of us have a few weeks of slaving left before our vacation."

"Welcome to the club!" I said, disappearing into the bathroom. A little later, I lay listening to the evening sounds outside: blackbirds yodeling in the treetops, and a cow that seemed to have something to say stubbornly mooing across the pastures. I thought about Coolie, standing in her box at the other side of the field. She'd probably just gotten her evening meal and was enjoying life to the max – my darling glutton! Sis was contentedly snuggled up in the hollow of my knee, snoring softly, her long, silky ears draped like some kind of flying appendages across the comforter. Her deep breaths made me drowsy, and while Disney characters jabbered away somewhere I slowly fell asleep.

Chapter 2

Although it felt early to get up at seven during summer vacation, it was a lot better than getting up that early for school. It was true that my bed felt wonderful, but not quite as wonderful as it felt on a rainy November morning. I quickly got dressed and took the dogs for a walk before I ran over to Vibeke's. The weather was better than it had been for weeks – although there were some gray-blue clouds here and there in the sky, a big stretch of it was actually blue and the sun generously shone through the morning haze.

In the stable, I was met by neighing and pawing. Hungry horses wanted their food – now! Vibeke had taken them inside last night to let them dry off after the rain, and also to make sure they got their portions of concentrated feed and certain vitamins. Every horse had his or her unique menu and everything was written on a board in the feed room. I could pick out Coolie's voice, a deep humming far down in her belly.

"Good morning, my darling," I twittered, and then I thought about what a good thing it is that people don't know how silly you can be when you're with your horse. Coolie was the first horse to be fed – I thought she should get some advantage from having her person work at the stable. I took the opportunity to scratch her a little behind her ears and caress her shoulder blade. Coolie turned her head, ears brushed back, as she always did when I tried to cuddle while she was eating. The horses didn't get any hay this time of year, as they were on their way outside to feast on juicy summer grass.

Once I got everybody outside it was time to muck out. I filled the wheelbarrow and pushed it out to the dunghill to empty it. My hands had hard calluses and I could tell that my arms had gotten stronger during my first year in Skåne.

"Breakfast is ready!" I heard Vibeke calling across the yard and quickly put my shovel away. By now, my belly was burning with hunger.

In the kitchen, the smell of toast and blackcurrant tea mixed with coffee was heavenly. I don't drink coffee, but I thought that the smell was wonderful. I quickly jumped into my usual place on the kitchen sofa. Vibeke's little Jack Russells were whirling around and play-fighting at my feet. Vibeke was holding Isa over her shoulder and drinking coffee with her free hand. Her hair, which used to be cut in as short, spiky 'do, had grown out a few inches, making her look a little softer. Yes, there actually was something soft and motherly about Vibeke, something that hadn't been there at all before she had Isa. I had seen this in our setters when they had given birth for the first time, a warm wisdom in their eyes that hadn't been there before. Isa's little round head was covered with golden down and her little back moved in small, quick breaths.

"Well, let's see what we have on our schedule for today. You can go with Jörgen to put up wire around the paddock closest to the woods; the poles are already in place."

I nodded, pushing half a sandwich into my mouth. Jörgen clattered in, wearing wooden clogs and blue pants full of straw.

"Good morning, girls. So, you're just sitting here being lazy!" Jörgen said to tease us, pouring a big cup of coffee for himself. Jörgen almost always had a big smile and some funny comment. Usually, Vibeke scolded him in a kind of loving way.

"Hey, you lout of a husband! Must you always come inside with mucky shoes on, and half a haystack stuck to your clothes? Did you hire a cleaning lady, or are you planning to vacuum this up yourself?"

"Oh, now she's being sarcastic too," Jörgen laughed, going out to the hallway to get rid of his shoes and half a haystack. Vibeke rolled her eyes and shook her head.

"Men – you can't live with them and you aren't allowed to shoot them!" she said, although with Vibeke's Danish accent, her Swedish wasn't too easy to make out.

"After lunch, I thought we might exercise Amaryllis and Tartan, and we can drive Spotlight a little too."

A little later, Jörgen and I were putting up electrical wire on the poles. I had to wear thick work gloves to keep the wire from cutting into my hands. It wasn't easy to get the wire properly tight, and sometimes it felt like there was some invisible weight attached to it. On top of that, I managed to walk through some poison ivy and earned a rash on my legs. For once, the sun had come out, and it was beating down on my bare shoulders. It gave me a sunburn but also felt nice and summery.

It took us so long to finish that we were almost late for lunch, and now that the weather was fine we took the opportunity to sit outside to eat, under the umbrella. I waged war against the flies that wouldn't stop landing on my food. A great drawback of living in the country was all the aggressive flies that never gave up and crept around on food, horses and people.

I didn't even want to think about where else they had been crawling as I ate.

"Now, don't forget the mosquito net on the wagon, there's milk in the fridge, and she's had her vitamin A and D drops." Vibeke always had a long list of instructions for Jörgen when she and I went to exercise the horses.

"Get out!" Jörgen shooed Vibeke away. "I've taken care of my own daughter before, haven't I!"

"Okay, okay, stop pushing me. Bye, bye, little sugar." Vibeke kissed Isa on her forehead and Jörgen closed the door behind us. I was the first to reach the tack room to change into riding pants and boots. My clothes had been spotted with mud since Maddie and I galloped on the woodland road. I tried to brush the mud off, but it mostly turned into a gray film of dust on my dark blue riding pants.

When we came out to the paddocks, Coolie went and stood by the gate expectantly. My heart really hurt when I took Amaryllis out and left Coolie there with ears pricked and head high.

"You can come later, honey!" I promised her.

We tied the horses in the passageway and prepared them for riding. I groomed Amaryllis, who stood with her head hanging, blinking sleepily. Her coat was like shiny velvet over her well-toned muscles. Blood vessels snaked

29

under her skin like some complicated river system on a map. I leaned the tip of my nose against her neck, enjoying the smell of sun-warmed horse, a little dusty and sweet. It was a safe, familiar smell that had been my favorite for years. Better than Chanel, Dior and any world-famous brands of perfume. Amaryllis obediently lifted one foot at a time so that I could pick them out. All Vibeke's horses had well-tended, fine feet. The frog was nice and firm and the hoof well-shaped and newly shod. My Coolie had had some problems with her hooves, which easily became dry and cracked, but since Vibeke gave me the tip to rub hand lotion into them they had actually gotten better. It was hard to get new shoes on her, too, and the farrier worked up a sweat when he, to my great horror, worked on her hooves until they bled.

I put on the tendon boots and brushing boots. In the beginning, I knew nothing about all the different kinds of protection and blankets. I discovered a whole jungle of accessories that I'd never used on Sesame, and that Vibeke seemed to know forwards and backwards by heart. I hadn't even been able to tell the difference between a pair of tendon boots and fetlock boots. Now, I can quickly get the boots on without having to stop and consider which goes on which leg.

"OK, let's do our usual twenty-minute warm-up," Vibeke said as she lithely jumped onto Tartan, who started eagerly treading in place, tail lifted proudly. I lengthened the leathers since Maddie, whose legs were a little shorter than mine, had ridden him last. She'd shortened them even more than usual for our trail ride. Soon, we'd be riding a chaos of tracks, in circles, serpentines and lines going in every direction.

Amaryllis's rocky gait made me sway in the saddle. She was lovely to ride, even if I always longed a little for Coolie when I was riding another horse. Every time her hoof hit the ground a little cloud of dust rose up. The day's warm, sunny weather had dried the top layer on the riding track.

We trotted around on loose reins and let the horses jog themselves warm. They snorted from the whirling dust and waved their tails at the flies. I felt relaxed and safe on Amaryllis's back, and Vibeke happily hummed some song that I didn't recognize. Right then, in the middle of our idyllic ride, I heard a dull sound on Amaryllis's rib cage and felt myself falling, then watched in surprise as Amaryllis headed in a very different direction from the one we had been going. I saw her bouncing, broad hindquarters gallop toward the stable while I sat, shocked, in the sand, staring after her like an idiot.

"What …! What happened? Are you okay?" Vibeke trotted up to me and slid off Tartan, landing just a couple of feet from me. At the same time, I heard shrill voices

31

rounding the corner of the stable, and several people shouting and laughing.

"Somebody threw something at us; look at that, isn't that an apple?" I pointed to something round and green, lying on the ground a few yards away.

"Hold Tartan. I'll run after Amaryllis before she gets tangled in her own reins." Vibeke disappeared with long bounds and I managed to get up from the sand in a somewhat embarrassing posture. Tartan was dancing around, excited by his stable friend's sudden outburst. I suppose he too would have loved to gallop off.

I went over to the green apple and discovered that it was a tennis ball. Who could be stupid enough to throw a tennis ball at a horse? I balanced on my toes to get a better view of the gravel road that was winding between fields and pastures, but the only thing I saw was the pig farmer on his tractor. He would hardly find it amusing to throw tennis balls at me.

"Amaryllis is all right!" Vibeke came walking with the beautiful chestnut mare. I felt relieved that she wasn't hurt or frightened by the "tennis ball attack."

"Up in the saddle again, Anna!"

"Did you see who it was? I heard some voices behind the stable."

"No idea. I didn't have time to see anything, but I thought I heard some boys' voices too. I guess it was a few bored teenagers. Well, let's walk a little on two tracks."

I collected Amaryllis, as well as myself. I started doing some circle tracks and made sure she was bent, and just when I was satisfied that she was bending nicely, Vibeke said, "Make sure she doesn't bend too much. You should be able to see her eyes and nostrils."

I straightened Amaryllis and concentrated on bending her the way Vibeke had explained. We did volts of different sizes at both trot and gallop, and I could feel a drop of sweat running between my shoulder blades. The shining coat on Amaryllis's neck got darker from sweat and the reins started slipping between my warm hands. We rode halfway through and did leg-yielding out to the long side.

"Move your inside leg up a little, Anna. She's leading with her hindquarters right now; don't forget that her front should lead her movements. Right, Anna, that's better!" Vibeke gave me a thumbs up before she made Tartan turn in a balanced and elegant leg-yielding. Vibeke's long, thin legs just seemed to brush at his sides and she looked so infuriatingly relaxed in the saddle. I wished that someday I'd be as good a rider as Vibeke. Personally, I felt like every lap at working trot or collected trot was a hard, uneven struggle. Before I knew it, I'd jolted and it took half a lap before I found my rhythm again and felt like I was floating with the movement. Sometimes I had to do a few laps of easy riding just because I got so tired from concentrating on sitting nicely down at a trot. Then, I had to keep tabs on my outside leg, which suddenly became my inside leg when I prepared for the yielding; dressage certainly wasn't all that easy!

"Sit straight on your horse, right, like that! Look where you're going, easy on the inner rein. There you go, that's the way to do it!"

All at once, I felt light as a feather, and Amaryllis worked forwards and answered all my aids almost before I gave them. We had a short moment of happiness when everything felt perfect, and I just smiled. This was my reward for hours in the saddle, rivers of sweat, frozen toes, riding sores and hurting muscles. All that drudgery for years and years just disappeared when riding took you to a small cloud of happiness where everything was just right. You felt like a mix between Isabell Werth and Ludwig Beerbaum, two of Sweden's top riders.

Blinded by my fairy-tale riding intoxication, I didn't watch where I was going and almost crashed into Vibeke and Tartan. Amaryllis threw her head up and jumped a little and I thudded down sadly, completely off balance … and the magic was gone.

34

"We drive on the right side here, you know," Vibeke laughed. "She really walked beautifully just now, very nice!"

I absorbed her praise like a dry sponge in a bucket full of water. Vibeke was careful about correcting your mistakes, but when you did a good job you always heard that too, and it was like music to my ambitious rider's ears. I really wanted to learn and get good, but it was so very much harder than it looked. The more I learned, the more I understood that I really didn't know quite as much as I thought I did.

We walked the horses a little to calm them down. I sat dangling my legs without stirrups and now and then I tugged at the neckband of my shirt, trying to cool myself by blowing air in there.

"I think we'll have thunder; it really feels oppressive," Vibeke said, squinting at the clouds that were towering over the horizon. It certainly was sultry; an unmoving heat seemed to suck the oxygen out of the air. I took a bucket of water and a sponge and washed Amaryllis's neck, which was tangled from dried sweat. She seemed to enjoy the water running from her neck and down over shoulders and legs. She was standing with her head low and eyes half-closed, her ears seeming to lose strength and turning a little outward, like on a donkey.

"You really like this, don't you? Your own spa with

private staff; that's something, huh?" I squeezed the water out of the sponge over her withers and back, which were also dark from sweat.

After we'd let Tartan and Amaryllis out in the paddock it was time to longe Spotlight. I always felt a little worried about managing Spotlight. He was quite unpredictable and very full of energy. Even if he didn't mean to hurt anybody, you could often be pushed, treaded on or kicked by him. Vibeke and Maddie were so unafraid and used to taking care of horses like that, while I became clumsy and uncertain when he started fussing.

Vibeke put the longe line on and I helped her with the chaps. Spotlight reared a little when we came out of the stable, made stallion movements with his head and neighed like crazy.

"Teenage boys!" Vibeke laughed. "You'd better pull yourself together, Spotty, you know the slaughterer's van passes here every Thursday."

She patted him lovingly. We often joked about the slaughterer's van and hamburgers, just because Spotlight could really test your patience, but everybody knew that Spotlight was one of the most promising young stallions that Vibeke had ever had, and his gaits were something to die for. So the slaughterer's van passed without Spotlight, and the stallion went on working toward the title of Baddest Boy in the Stable.

Vibeke stood in the middle with Spotty trotting around her. I perched on the fence and tried to learn as much as I could. Vibeke explained to me about form and shortening the line while she almost imperceptibly did small things with the line, making him bend and go low. As usual, Spotlight did some happy capers now and then, but as soon as he started walking for real he was a total thing of beauty. His white blaze sloped down his beautiful, Thoroughbred-like head. He looked like his mother, Amaryllis, so powerful but still slender. His coloring was like his dad's, Fraser Tartan, a lovely Thoroughbred from Ireland with a dark, chestnut brown coat and black legs. Frase, as he was called, was on loan to a three-day event rider who competed at the elite level, and Frase had placed himself high both in Sweden and abroad. I had seen a DVD of Frase walking a cross-country track in England. My hands broke out in a sweat just watching it; the obstacles were fixed and enormous. There was jumping going downhill, going uphill, and from totally hopeless angles. Disaster seemed to loom just inches away all the time and I quickly decided that I was not going to be a three-day event rider at elite level!

I tried handling the longe line for a while, and it felt very strange to be able to influence the horse only from the ground and not give leg aids or use my body weight. It was harder than I thought to balance the horse just with longe, but at the same time, it was fun to see the entire horse while I was working with it.

When we were done with Spotlight it was past three and I could feel my body starting to protest all the physical exertion. I had been on the go since early morning, only sitting down for a few minutes during breakfast. I decided that Coolie could have a day off, so that I could go home and relax for a while. Tomorrow would be another day of hard work; the stable needed to be pressure washed and Maddie had promised to come and help out.

At home, there was an unnatural calm. Mom was at work and Jonatan and Kalle were at the daycare center until around five. I sat in the garden with a giant glass of apple juice and a pack of crackers. Sis and Malou ran around the garden, sniffing at molehills or chasing each other for fun. They were glad that somebody was finally home. I was filled with guilt and fed them crackers to ease my conscience. It was nice finally just to sit down and take it easy, and I leafed through a few magazines that I'd bought a week before. Nothing new, just the same old celebrities dieting themselves down to size zero, looking all weird. Sometimes I thought that I was a little too thin, but I was almost flabby compared to their bony, sharp bodies. Advice about makeup and new fashion of course were lost on me. My daily wardrobe consisted of shorts or riding pants, and I made my face up maybe three times a year. Sometimes, Mom and I decided to change the color of our hair and helped each other to become "warm auburn" or "hot hazelnut." That was where my beauty regime ended. My hands weren't even worth mentioning; my nails are always chipped, and I have calloused palms and chapped skin. I decided that my role as a horse owner made it impossible to keep up fashion-magazine standards when it came to beauty care!

Chapter 3

The rumbling started around ten, still sounding muffled and distant. Mom was lying on the sofa, dressed in a white bathrobe, with a turban of terry cloth around her head and her toenails freshly painted. Somebody in the family seemed to remember their beauty care, after all.

"Anna, honey, will you walk the dogs tonight?" Mom asked with a velvety voice. I knew that she was feeling quite cozy on her sofa, newly bathed and painted, and didn't feel like going out into a thunderstorm with threatening rain clouds. I sighed loudly but thought that it just might be a good thing to collect bonus points with Mom, and besides, Sis was actually my responsibility. I put my bare feet into a pair of green rubber boots and slipped on a rain jacket; best to be prepared. The dogs were in ecstasy, as usual.

"Easy now, girls! Try to control yourselves just a little." We spilled out through the door. The two setters ran away in a merry gallop, ears flapping around their heads. Dramatic clouds moved across the sky in an ominous way, giving the summer night a gray-blue sheen. Heavy raindrops, still just a few of them, fell down on my jacket with small splashes. In spite of the rain, the air was hot, creating condensation inside my jacket. It wasn't very fun to live in the middle of a countryside that was off limits. The farmers watched protectively and attacked you for the smallest little hoof print at the edge of a field. I couldn't understand why it was such a terrible thing if a horse happened to tread on a field, making one little mark, but to the farmers, it seemed to mean life or death for the year's harvest.

Right now, the dogs were actually making small excursions into the fields, but I hoped that little dog's prints would be invisible, or maybe that the farmer would think that the prints hade been made by foxes or something, since it was totally impossible to keep the dogs on the road without a leash – and leashes were such a drag with two lively setters.

Suddenly, the silence was broken by an unmistakable sound: agitated barking in falsetto – dogs on a rabbit hunt.

41

"Oh, no! Sis, Malouuu!" I yelled futilely in the darkness. I squinted, trying to make out something in the twilight. The barking receded and I could tell that the dogs were already at least halfway to the next town.

After calling out and whistling for almost fifteen minutes, I finally saw something moving ahead of me on the road. Malou came running up to me, puffing like a bellows.

"So, where's Sis?" I asked, putting Malou on a leash just in case she tried to make a break for more rabbit hunting. Malou looked at me with her tongue hanging like a tie and her ears pricked. If she knew where her naughty daughter was, she didn't seem to want to tell me. I turned into our little driveway and saw the welcoming lights in the window panes of our whitewashed house. The honeysuckle wound around the front door like a piece of jewelry and smelled sweet, almost like vanilla.

"That was some long walk! I almost got worried," I heard my mom call from the living room.

"Sis is out rabbit hunting. I have to go look for her," I said, turning Malou loose.

"It's almost eleven thirty. Don't you think it's a little late to go out? You stay with the kids and I'll take the car and try to find her," Mom suggested, rising from the sofa.

"Oh, what could happen out here in the boondocks? She always comes when I whistle. I'll take my phone, just in case." I disappeared out in the darkness, carrying a flashlight to see better. The rain had ended and the strange warmth, almost like some kind of sauna, kept its grip and made me sweat although it was almost the middle of the night. I thought I'd better go over to the big road in case she was wandering around there. My greatest fear was to find her run down by a car somewhere.

I heard something and stopped to listen. The sound came from the farm just before the big road. Maybe it was Sis, and she'd found a playmate. That farm was full of dogs, cats and little pony foals. I turned into the little driveway. I saw something move in the darkness, but the something was a lot bigger than dogs: horses. Two figures had mounted two of the horses in the paddock, and it seemed as if they were trying to urge the horses to gallop by hitting and waving with halter-chains. I couldn't make out their faces but could see that they seemed to be somewhat older kids, maybe in their early teens. The laughter I heard through the night air seemed somehow familiar; maybe I had heard it on the school bus sometime.

It felt embarrassing to sneak around like this in the middle of the night, so I decided to turn around – Sis was obviously not here. Strange people, going out in a thunderstorm at this time of night to ride their horses. And also, they seemed to treat their horses in a mean way.

I turned my flashlight on and let the beam play across the fields. It felt a little uncanny to wander around all by myself, and I missed the safety of having the dogs around. When I came to the big road, I whistled and called out as loudly as I could. My voice seemed so lonely and puny when it cut through the darkness. It felt like I was all alone in the world (except for two loonies out for some rowdy riding in the middle of the night). When my cell rang I jumped one foot up in the air and my heart made a backwards somersault in my chest; I'd forgotten that I had it in my pocket.

"Sis is home now. I'll have to put her in the shower; she's totally muddy! You want me to pick you up with the car?" It was Mom calling – I could see Sis in my mind's eye, mud hanging from her coat and her tail going like a propeller. A weight fell from my chest and I could breathe a little easier; it was always a little creepy when the dogs ran away and you didn't know what was going to happen to them. Besides, in the latest weeks the papers had featured articles about nasty people who kidnapped dogs and sold them for who knows what purpose. I had had a movie about fur farms mailed to me and it was the worst thing I'd ever seen; dogs being used to make fur coats. I started crying helplessly when I watched it and regretted clicking the "Order Now" icon on the website.

When I got home, I was met by a sweet-smelling Sis,

who seemed to think that she had had a great night out of hunting, mud wrestling and shampooing. Of course, Mom didn't look quite as fresh as when I'd left her. Her bathrobe was full of muddy paw prints and her hair was standing in all directions after bending over Sis. I decided that Sis would sleep in the hallway, to keep my bed from getting wet, and then quickly realized that I would have to get up and go to work in less than seven hours …

The time had come for a thorough spring cleaning. The entire stable was to be emptied and cleaned. Vibeke, Jörgen, Maddie and I were standing by ready, like warriors before a battle, armed with high-pressure washers, assorted powders and cleaning agents for dirt, fungus, fly maggots and other nasty things that we didn't want to cultivate in the stable.

Jörgen started patiently emptying wheelbarrow after wheelbarrow of the boxes, while we girls carried everything from the tack room, the feed room and the passageway out on the yard. We struggled with stable boxes, piles of blankets, riding clothes and everything else that a stable is filled with. The air felt a little fresher and lighter after the thunderstorm, something that we all were thankful for as we toiled, carried and lifted until our arms ached. I screamed loudly when I pulled out a barrel of horse muesli and two mice scuttled across the concrete floor.

"Easy now; that was just two little mice. Wait until the rats come out; they're bigger than dogs," Jörgen teased me with a wink. I carefully scrutinized him, but I could never tell if he was making fun of me or just stating a fact that he considered funny.

Outside, once we emptied the stable, it looked like we were holding an enormous yard sale. We all helped to sweep out all the boxes and the passageway. The stable echoed desolately and I realized how much nicer a place it was when it was full of horses. I've always felt that stables are at their coziest in the winter. It feels so snug and sheltered when all the horses are in there, chewing hay. You can hear the comfortable grinding of their jaws. I love the cozy feeling of snuggling with my horse while the snow whirls outside.

All the dust in the air made me sneeze, so I was happy to see Jörgen starting the high-pressure washer and attacking the furniture, walls and ceilings. Cascades of water exploded against the stone walls and ran in gray-green rivers down to the draining-well. Maddie and I took care of the stable windows, cleaning the panes until it looked as if they weren't there at all. We even took the wet vac vacuum cleaner and dusted all of Vibeke's competition plaques, which were covering the walls. On them, you could read names and places of the hundreds of competitions that she'd placed high in. It was impressive to see how many there were and from how many different towns in the country they came. A few were also from Denmark, Germany, Holland and other places in Europe. In the tack room, we wiped faded framed photos of Vibeke wearing a dressage hat and dress coat, sitting on beautiful, calm dressage horses. At the farm, she mostly wore big sweaters and worn-out boots, so I was totally fascinated by the pictures of her dressed up for competitions. In one picture, she had really long hair, collected beautifully in a net.

"I wonder if I'll ever get to ride like that ..." I soared away in competition fantasies.

"Well, you did well this spring," Maddie said, optimistic as always. She was an "every-cloud-has-a-silver-lining" kind of girl.

"Yeah, right! A silly Easy C at the Omset trials," I sulked. Maddie laughed at me.

"Well, you were pretty satisfied at the time, as I remember it!"

And she was right. It had been my first dressage competition. I was riding Disa, I was ready to throw up from nerves and my knees shook so terribly that I thought they could be heard all the way up to the stands. Nice, friendly Disa didn't take any notice of the nervous wreck on her back but obeyed my shaky aids and did all I asked for. We ended up in fourth place and got a ribbon as well as a lap of honor. I was silly with happiness and forever grateful that I hadn't thrown up or fainted in the saddle. I smiled at the memory.

"Hope I can ride Coolie next time."

"Course you can! We can put in our names for Omset's summer competitions. They have both jumping and dressage." Maddie looked at me with a hopeful smile.

"Yes, wouldn't that be fun," I said, as perky as I could. Just the words "put in our names" sounded so final and definitive that I got a dizzy feeling in my belly. Competitions were always best in your imagination, where you rode like a god and always won blue and yellow ribbons. Also, in my imagination I never felt sick or got sweaty hands and heart failure.

The horses stood curiously in a row and watched our efforts. I suspected that they were hoping some friendly soul would carry the fodder barrels out and pour the contents on the ground in front of them. Spotlight scratched his forelegs like an angry bull and neighed urgently. As usual, Vibeke's mares were standing in a little trio of their own, and for once they weren't gnawing at each other's withers or waving flies away from each other. Coolie, also as usual, was standing alone, a little apart, and my heart ached when I saw her all alone. Vibeke used to comfort me by saying that Coolie seemed to enjoy being by herself, and she actually never tried to make friends with any of the other mares, who didn't take any notice of her anymore. Still, I wished that she had a friend who would gnaw at her withers and wave away flies.

I couldn't resist my horse and took a break from cleaning and crawled under the fence to Coolie. She quickly frisked me to see if I had some goodies on me.

"You sweet tooth," I cooed softly. "I guess you're always hungry; even though you have acres of food right under your feet, you still have to beg for more." I scratched her behind her ears, knowing that she liked that. For a few seconds she stood very still with her head pressed against me, but then she must have felt that she had had enough of such silliness, since she shook her head violently and started to graze.

"Ice cream break!" Jörgen waved with a few ice cream cones. I hurried over and grabbed one. We had worked hard, and I was very hungry. We sat down on the garden furniture, which stood by the stable wall. Roses wound their way up a trellis on the whitewashed wall. The dark red flowers smelled sweet. The sun was out and a few swallows danced high in the sky in a breakneck air show. The grass was yellow with dandelions. It was a little more than one week to midsummer and the summer was so wonderfully warm and bright that it felt like it would never end. I just wanted to stop time, and make everything be like this forever: sun, horses, ice cream and no tedious to-do list. Of course my body was aching after an entire morning of cleaning, my hair felt thick with dust and my legs were striped by dirty water, which had run down from the windows while we were washing them. But who cared, now that school was out and summer was ahead of us!

Vibeke had disappeared inside with Isa, who had wakened and informed everybody that she was hungry. Jörgen stomped into the empty and echoing stable to finish his high-pressure washing and Maddie and I had to get up and clean all the side rooms. It was unbelievable how much dust and spiderwebs were everywhere, even if I still thought Vibeke's stable was the cleanest one I'd ever seen. We took a lunch break and then went back to work until almost five.

"The horses can go outside at night now that the weather's good. I'll prepare the foal box, so Mona and Disa can come in at night." Jörgen was standing in the doorway to the tack room where we were rubbing the last spots from the shelves where the riding helmets were stored. Jörgen's cheeks were glowing from hard work and he was all spotty from the high-pressure washer.

"Good," I said, wiping sweat from my forehead with the sleeve of my T-shirt. "That means there's only one box to muck out and that suits me fine, because I feel as fresh and alert as this rag!" I waved a very used rag in front of me.

"Oh come now, nobody's died from a little work! You two little delicate flowers need some exercise," Jörgen teased, grinning mischievously. I was much too tired to sass him back, but at least I managed to throw the rag, which landed on his shoulder with a smacking wet sound.

"So, that's how it is!" Jörgen put the muzzle of the high-pressure washer on his hip and looked like Clint Eastwood ready to fire. Maddie and I ran out of the stable, screaming as if a murderer was after us, and just when I was out of the door I was hit by a hard water jet that almost burned the small of my back. The water was icy cold and totally drowned me in a few seconds. Maddie also got her share, and she stood there frozen, arms out from her body, gasping for breath.

"Th-th-that w-w-w-was cold!" she stammered, water running in rivulets down on the gravel below the stable window.

"Well, think of it this way; now you won't have to shower tonight, girls!" Jörgen waved to us with a happy and triumphant grin on his face before disappearing into the stable again.

"This means revenge!" I declared while wringing water from my ponytail.

"Absolutely. B-big fat revenge," Maddie said, shoulders shaking from her shivering.

We staggered homewards in our wet clothes and I realized that I'd even forgotten to say goodbye to Coolie. When we finally made it to my house, we took turns taking long hot showers. It's unbelievable how certain showers in your life can become almost spiritual experiences. I showered for so long, and the water was so hot, that I couldn't even see the furniture in the bathroom through the fog. I shampooed my hair twice and scrubbed myself with a loofah. When I was finally done and I opened the bathroom door, steam belched out into the hall.

"Oh, you've got a steam bath – that's great!"

"It does become a steam bath if you shower a long time and the water's hot enough, but my guess is by now there's only about half gallon of hot water left for you. Still, that shouldn't matter since you had a shower this afternoon anyway!"

"Ha ha ha, you're sooo funny." Maddie disappeared into the fog and the door closed.

After freshening up, we sat in the garden with chocolate milk and sandwiches. I felt as if I could devour an entire loaf of bread, and I actually tried to. Afterwards, I reclined in the garden chair, enjoying the evening sun and the perfect cooler evening temperature. The dogs played with Konrad, our kitten that soon would be more

52

grown-up cat than kitten. Konrad hid under flowers and bushes and then jumped out like a pouncing tiger, attacking the passing dogs. The dogs loved the game and let him attack them over and over again.

"We have to go to the midsummer party in Lyby," Maddie said in a decisive tone that made it clear that she had already made her mind up, for both of us.

"What party?" I looked at Maddie in surprise. Her black hair was combed back after her shower, and shined almost blue-black in the sun.

"You know, midsummer: herring, dancing around the pole, lots of mosquitoes? Swedish midsummer."

"Will there be one of those lame dance bands playing?"

"Of course! If there weren't, it wouldn't be a real midsummer, would it?"

I sighed somewhat dejectedly, even though it might be fun. It wasn't as if I'd been going to lots of dances this last year. I'd kind of put boys totally on the back burner, so to speak. Sometimes, I felt a little buzz when I happened to see some real cute guy, but my horse took up so much time, and school. It didn't really feel as if there was room for boys after all that. And anyway, what guy would be interested in a girl like me? I always smelled like a horse, never wore make-up, and dressed in practical, barn-style clothes. At home, I had two impossible twin brothers who never left me alone, and anyway, I hadn't even kissed a boy in almost a year, so I hardly remembered how to do it …

"Hmm … I wonder if I should wear a dress or just jeans …" Maddie wrinkled her brow and looked as if she was pondering a new cure for cancer.

Chapter 4

Maddie stayed over that night and we got up early. We took our summer job at Vibeke's very seriously, since we were actually getting paid. It was the first time in my life that I was actually paid to take care of horses. For years and years I'd toiled and drudged just to be close to them.

When we approached Vibeke's farm, I got one of those uncanny feelings that something wasn't right. I quickly scanned the paddocks to check that the horses were there. The number of horses was right, but still something felt wrong. In the mares' paddock, the horses were running around the long side of the fence, and they seemed upset, as if a predator were lying in wait behind the bushes. The guys on the other side of the fence also seemed restless and worried.

"Maybe an elk ran through the paddock," Maddie said, squinting at the hazy fields.

"I just hope nobody's hurt." I took longer steps to get there faster. Surprised, I stopped and picked up a lead rein that was lying on the yard.

"That's strange, we hung up every lead rein yesterday. How did this get here?"

"Maybe Jörgen dropped it when he was taking Disa and the foal in," Maddie said, searching for some logical explanation to ease my worry.

I bent down and sneaked into the paddock where the mares were. Cissi trotted up to me and I drew my hand across her back in fright.

"What's this? Look at this, Maddie; she has marks, as if somebody's been riding her! Look at her hindquarters – there are marks from some kind of crop or something!" I was seized with fear. We examined Cissi from top to bottom without finding anything else.

"Oh no, Amaryllis is bleeding!" Maddie drew her hand over the horse's shinbone. There was a four-inch long gash close to the joint on the inside of her foreleg.

"Run in and get Jörgen and Vibeke! I'll check the rest of the horses."

Maddie was off like a shot and I hurried to the next

horse. To my great relief I couldn't see any marks on Coolie. I examined every inch of her, and even lifted all four legs to check under her hooves. I kissed her forehead, relieved, and tenderly held my hands around her long ears.

Vibeke and Jörgen came running from the house. Little Isa was bouncing in a baby carrier against Jörgen's chest. Vibeke quickly checked all the horses with Jörgen at her side. We could see and hear that they both were very upset. When Vibeke got agitated, she forgot her Swedish entirely and spoke in hard-to-understand Danish, but at least I could understand that she was asking Jörgen to call the police. Jörgen quickly took his phone from his jeans pocket and moved a few yards off to talk.

"It seems they only rode Cissi and Amaryllis. I can't imagine why we didn't wake up! I know I heard the dogs barking a couple of times, but they do that every night when the cats dig in the flowerbeds.

"They must have taken the lead reins we hang on the gate and used those for reins. That way, they had something to beat the horses with, too – the swine!"

I could feel my face getting hot with anger. Who would do something like this? Ride a horse until it bleeds and then just leave it in that condition. I was almost sick with anger and loathing.

"What idiot sneaks out to a paddock in the middle of the night to ride horses without permission?" Vibeke exclaimed, angrily shaking her head.

Just at that moment, it struck me; what idiot sneaks out to a paddock in the middle of the night to ride horses without permission ... I suddenly remembered the night of the thunderstorm, when I'd been out looking for Sis.

"I think I might know who they are –" I began haltingly.

"What? You know who they are? Who?" Maddie and Vibeke spoke at the same time, staring at me with wide eyes.

"When I was looking for Sis, that night when there was a thunderstorm, I saw somebody riding at the farm close to the big road. It must be their kids who did this. They were riding like crazy, hitting the horses with something!"

"You mean Månsson's kids? Could that be possible?" Vibeke looked at me incredulously. "Would they really sneak into our yard and ride our horses? That seems so totally dumb. They have their own horses to ride."

"Yeah, but those kids seem more wild than tame. They gallop like madmen on the gravel roads. Maybe they've destroyed their own horses but want to ride anyway?" I knew that my theories were somewhat unformed, but it just couldn't be coincidence that they'd been riding exactly this same way just a few nights before. How many illicit nightly riders could there be in our little village?

"The police can't come for a few hours. I called the vet, too," said Jörgen as he came up and put his arm around Vibeke's shoulders. Vibeke rested her head on his chest and kissed Isa's cheek.

"Well, we'll make sure they're put away for this," Jörgen said decisively. "Now let's get Cissi and Amaryllis inside."

"I guess we'll have to go talk to the Månssons, too," Vibeke sighed, putting the lead rein on Amaryllis's dark brown head-collar.

Jörgen took out his digital camera and took pictures of every part of the horses that showed some mark from the riders, and also of their wounds. Vibeke carefully washed the wounds and put a bandage on Amaryllis's leg. The mood in the stable was subdued. Everybody was upset and angry about what had happened, and we didn't even know if the rider or riders planned to return.

"What if they come back and hurt the horses? I've read several stories about sick madmen breaking into stables just to hurt the horses!" The very thought made me shiver and I almost burst out crying.

Jörgen patted my shoulder and said, "Easy now, I'll make sure not even a hedgehog can get into the yard. Even if I have to sit on the porch with my shotgun!"

Vibeke couldn't help laughing at that. "Well, that would certainly be a sight; you running around with your shotgun, aiming for hedgehogs!"

"But they're so cute!" I exclaimed, defending the hedgehogs.

"Piles of fleas with needles are what they are!" Jörgen exclaimed forcefully enough to make everybody laugh. It was a relief to be able to laugh in this awful situation.

The vet arrived and examined the horses. She did some bending tests out in the yard and assigned me the task of running with the horses to see if they were lame. Luckily, their worst problems seemed to be some scratch wounds on their legs and marks from being beaten with a broken-off tree branch or some kind of crop.

Then the police came to file a report about what had happened. They asked millions of questions, and once again I had to tell what I had seen and heard up at the Månssons' place a couple of nights ago. It felt unreal to stand there and talk about that night with a policeman in uniform – kind of serious, somehow. The police were going up to talk to the Månssons on their way home and I felt like a snitch that everybody would hate. I did tell the police that I wasn't sure that the Månssons' kids were the ones who had been riding Vibeke's horses, but still, I had to tell what I had seen.

Maddie and I rode Coolie and Tartan at a slow walk. It was windy, and the clouds hurried across the sky as if they were on their way somewhere and were already late. The wind made the horses perk up a little, jump with feet together for almost no reason and start to jig-jog. I had to collect Coolie and sit deeply in the saddle before I could let the loose reins again.

"I'm so glad I have Shotster! He's so small and easy to get up on," Maddie said.

Maybe that's why they didn't take Coolie; she doesn't look too easy to ride bareback, I thought thankfully.

"You really think it was the Månssons' kids?"

Maddie watched me carefully. I shrugged and shook my head.

"I actually don't know … but it certainly was weird that they were out riding that night."

"I really hope they get them," Maddie said emphatically. The only sounds we heard were the creaking of our saddles and the whispering wind. We rode, quiet and thoughtful, and didn't even care about the gallop stretch the way we usually did. The horses started trotting expectantly and shook their heads in exasperation when we reined them in. They were used to galloping on that straight stretch and probably thought that we were really boring.

We had almost made it back to the stable when a trotting sulky came up behind us. The driver was Christian from the Lindvalls' trotting stable. He liked to exercise his horses out in the gravel roads and he always stopped to talk a little. He had this unbelievable ability to make me embarrassed and go all red in the face. Christian was good-looking, blond, and had broad shoulders and a real toothpaste commercial smile. That aside, he was actually pretty nice, which made everything even more embarrassing. He probably thought that I was a great big nerd. Maddie knew him, since her stepdad was a trotting trainer, so when Maddie was with me they always chatted for a long time. The rumor of the police visiting Vibeke's farm had already spread, and of course people wanted to know why.

"Well, I'll be darned," Christian said when he heard what had happened. "I've heard stories about madmen who go in and hurt horses. I guess we'll have to watch our horses extra carefully now.

"Anyway, I guess I'd better get home before sundown; I have two more horses to drive," he then said after we had chatted for quite a while.

"See you in Lyby next Friday, then. Bye!"

Christian slapped his reins on the hindquarters of the horse, which immediately shot off at a trot.

"So, will he be going to the midsummer party?" I asked, trying to sound as if I wasn't very interested.

"He's always there; his father usually handles the grill. Maybe you'd be interested in dancing cheek to cheek?" Maddie smiled impishly and winked her right eye twice with her mouth wide open. It looked so silly that I had to laugh.

"You're so lame, Maddie! I'm not interested. I have no time for guys now, anyway."

"Well well, the old defense speech. 'I have no time for guys.' I understand, I completely understand."

Maddie kept teasing me, laughing smugly. I just smiled and shook my head, sighing deeply. Christian was really cute, but in a naturally charming way, as if he didn't make any effort at all.

When we slid off the horses outside the stable, Jörgen came up to us.

"The police phoned again. The Månssons were at a birthday party, kids and all, and didn't come home until one thirty in the morning," he explained.

"But didn't they notice anything about the horses?" I asked while I drew the stirrups up and pulled the leathers through.

"No, but I guess they're not too finicky about their horses. It's mostly their kids who look after them."

"So, who could it be?" Maddie seemed to be talking mostly to herself. She unsnapped Tartan's noseband and scratched his muzzle by his lower lip.

"We'll just have to be very observant, and you two make sure you keep your cell phones on in case you see anything."

Jörgen sauntered toward his beloved tractor, swung up into it easily and drove away, dust flying.

Maddie and I tied our horses up in the passageway. We brushed and groomed them carefully. Although grooming wasn't really necessary, it felt nice to have something to do. I greased Coolie's hooves and sprayed her with fly repellant. Coolie was fond of being groomed but seemed to like it even more when I finally snapped her fly mask on to protect her eyes against bugs and let her out onto the green pasture. She filled her mouth with grass and then lay down to rub her back for a while.

During the following days, phones rang nonstop and everybody was on the Internet to get the latest news. It turned out that a stable a few miles away had also had visitors. An Icelandic horse had been hurt when somebody tried to jump it over a junk pile outside the paddock where the horse was kept. The horse owners in the area were becoming more and more scared. There were false rumors that the horses that had been ridden also had been hurt with knives and had had their tails cut off. Everybody started suspecting everybody else, meaning that even more strange rumors were spread in the vein of, "I heard somebody saying that …" – with no evidence to back up the rumor.

Maddie and I discussed the whole thing over and over again. If we hadn't had our stable job in the daytime I guess we would have gone crazy. The days when Maddie was home at her own farm, I had to take care of the stable

and the horses by myself. I weeded the flowerbeds, put
new straw into the boxes, and helped Jörgen scrape doors
and windows that were to be repainted. There was no rest
and no peace.

Then, Maddie and I had to find some time to ride.
We had agreed to be in some competitions during
the summer, so we had to practice both jumping and
dressage. The dressage was Easy B, which really wasn't
that advanced, but we had to remember the entire
program and that actually wasn't easy. I ran around
by myself out on the yard, like when I was a little kid
playing at horses, and tried to memorize the track.

"You know, we have horses for that!" Jörgen called.
He was sitting on the roof like a giant crow in blue
overalls, painting the gables.

Vibeke, bless her, helped me out when I tried the
program on Coolie.

"I'll never manage all this hopeless working trot!" I
whimpered, wiping sweat off my forehead with the back
on my hand.

"Working trot is just what the doctor ordered, little
miss. Now let your knees down; you can't hug the horse
like that. Elastic wrists, softer hands, yes, that's right!"

I sat down at a trot, trying to make it look as if it
wasn't as uncomfortable as it really was. My dream was
a dressage program with mostly walking and galloping

65

and maybe a few short trotting exercises with a lot of easy riding! You would think that an Easy B would be a piece of cake, but in some strange way the very easiness of it was what made it hard. Reining backwards with impulsion – how could you have impulsion when you were supposed to walk backwards? It was hard to stand at a halt for six seconds and hold the horse in the correct posture all the time. And however strange it may sound, some parts of walking could also be hard to get right.

"Extended walk, Anna! You have to see a noticeable change from medium walk to extended walk. Hold her on the reins, but let her lengthen her neck a little. Don't move faster – her steps should become longer!"

With Vibeke as coach, both Coolie and I were soaked with sweat after one hour. I put Coolie in the water box and let the water play over her steaming body. She snorted and put her muzzle against the hose the whole time, making the water spurt in all directions. I was about as wet as Coolie when we were done.

At home there were complicated preparations, since Mom had decided to go to Uppsala with the twins. It was hard to believe, but she was letting me stay at the house alone all weekend, since Vibeke and Jörgen were close by if anything happened.

"Don't light any candles or anything, and lock the door carefully now that the dogs aren't here."

Mom had a million warnings and chores, and wrote lists to help me remember them all.

"Oh come on, Mom, I'm actually starting high school now, not fifth grade!" I complained, pushing her against the door. "You'd better go now, or you'll get there very late. Say hi to Grandma for me."

I hugged Kalle and Jonatan and got a long, hard hug from Mom.

"Promise to call if anything happens!"

"Yes, yes, yes. Stop nagging. Have a nice midsummer!"

Mom finally gave in, and when she had buckled my brothers into their car seats and put the dogs in their cages the car finally rolled off. I could see Malou's and Sis's eager setter faces in the rear window. They were fogging up the glass, panting happily.

I took Konrad in my arms and pressed him to my chest and throat. He answered immediately by starting to purr like a little moped engine.

"So, here we are all by our lonesome, Konrad. If you're good, you can share a bag of snacks with me tonight!"

Konrad rubbed his little nose against my cheek. He really loved snacks.

Chapter 5

On Midsummer's Eve I was off stable duty, and it felt like a real luxury to sleep in and not have to hurry to the stable. I had a peaceful breakfast on my own, toast and yogurt and cereal. The house felt almost a little spooky when I was alone. It was especially empty without the dogs – they had an unbelievable ability to fill the house, sort of like my twin brothers; they were always seen and heard.

After breakfast I decided to even out my tan. Mom used to tease my and say that I was a real redneck. My face and arms tanned but my feet, belly and back were white as chalk. I found my bikini and lay in the sun, which was, unfortunately, playing peek-a-boo. I was almost chilly every time it disappeared behind a cloud, and I kept throwing a blanket on and off every time. Lying there having a lazy time, and not even walking over to see to Coolie, felt almost like playing hooky.

My phone sang a silly ditty and I woke from my sun-induced trance.

"Dad will pick you up in an hour." It was Maddie calling. "So, what are you going to wear?"

I blinked against the white light in confusion and brushed off an ant that was wandering around on my shin.

"Wear?"

"Yeah, to the dance." Maddie sounded a little impatient. "Are you totally confused today?"

"Rightrightright, the dance. Well, um, I think I might wear jeans, in case there are a lot of mosquitoes."

"So what are you wearing with them?" Maddie pushed on, and it hit me that I had neither taken a shower nor chosen clothes and that her dad would be here in an hour.

"You know, I have to go check on my ironing!" It was a little white lie to get out of the conversation without having to admit that I'd totally forgotten about the party and was sleeping in the sun.

I quickly jumped in the shower, and when I wiped the steam off the mirror afterwards I could see that my shoulders and back were an angry red. I rubbed myself with a fragrant cream and actually made up my face for once. A little mascara and lip-gloss and a careful spray

69

of Mom's most expensive perfume: no horse-smell around here!

I jumped into a pair of clean jeans and a white top. It felt summer fresh and looked good against my tan. I was ready right when Maddie's dad honked outside.

Maddie wore a light yellow dress with thin straps and a ribbon under her chest. With her black hair and golden-brown skin she was incredibly cute. I was used to seeing her in dirty riding pants and a big T-shirt with some silly logo on it.

"You look great!" I exclaimed and hugged her. Maddie made a somewhat embarrassed face.

"Actually, it feels kind of weird; I don't strut around in a dress and sandals every day!" She demonstratively lifted a chubby, tanned foot in black straps. "And you look wonderful with your hair down and flattened like that!" Maddie ran her fingers through my nice-smelling hair and we laughed at ourselves. This was how most girls in the village looked every day, but for us it was solemn and almost religious.

The party grounds were full of people, there was already dancing around the midsummer pole and the music echoed over pastures and fields. We went around and bought a few lottery tickets, and we tried to win giant boxes of chocolate in different stands where you were supposed to hit cans with a ball or shoot down plastic ducks. I didn't win any chocolate, just a fiery orange and hairy little monkey that bounced on an elastic band. A little later a band started playing on the outdoor dance floor. It was just as I had feared – a handful of old men who, judging from their prominent bellies and furrowed faces, were soon going to reach retirement age, were playing "couples" songs that everybody seemed to know the words to. Maddie was quickly asked for a dance by some neighbor and it turned out she was great at couples dancing.

"Want to dance?" I suddenly heard a voice in my ear, so close that it was impossible to miss who was asking. I whirled around and met Christian's tanned face and a shrewd, blindingly white smile. I wasn't smart enough to say no, although I'd never danced this kind of dance, but mumbled "okay," and probably got all red in the face.

It was a hip-hop tune and Christian gave me my first lesson in hip-hop dancing. I felt like the first participant that had to leave, "So You Think You Can Dance?" He whirled me back and forth and suddenly rolled me into his arms to then throw me out at arm's length again. I got so dizzy that I took sidesteps and tripped on my own feet, but Christian just laughed.

After the dance, Christian bought me a soda and chatted with me for a while. It felt strangely natural to talk to him, and I don't even think I blushed. We talked about horses and gossiped about the neighboring farms. Christian told me that he had a summer job as a janitor at a home for criminal youths a few miles from Omset. I was grateful that I had my own summer job at Vibeke's, which made me avoid feeling like a little kid.

"Hey Christian, come on and dance with me; you can babysit some other day!" A girl with long blonde hair and big dangling silver earrings grabbed Christian's arm with her fake-nailed hands and dragged him off toward the dance floor. She smiled flirtatiously at Christian and didn't even bother to look at me.

"Easy, easy now, Jennie!" Christian turned to me and fired off a smile that made my stomach twitter.

"Thanks for the dance, Anna! Seems I have to go …"

I waved somewhat awkwardly and felt the words "babysit" burning in my brain. What a little gnat; how old could she be? No more than a couple of years older than I am, probably.

That was the only dance I got with Christian. For the rest of the evening a whole bunch of girls and boys that seemed to know each other well and kept to their little clan buzzed around him. Maddie and I were asked to dance anyway, and dance we did, from acne-faced nervous young boys to friendly old slow-moving farmers.

I got twenty-six mosquito bites.

Chapter 6

On Midsummer's day, we were back on stable duty, hair in ponytails and T-shirts with corporate logos – just as shabby as usual, in other words. Maddie's dad had brought Shotster up to Vibeke's farm so we could ride together.

Maddie and I decided to practice jumping and started dragging poles and fences around the riding ring. Under the arbor by the track, Jörgen was sitting with a big bottle of soda next to him and a cap pulled way down on his forehead. He was lounging in a chaise, and we couldn't really tell if he was asleep or not. Vibeke had told us that they had had friends over last night and Jörgen was exhausted. It felt weird to see Jörgen so out of it. Usually, he was like the battery rabbit, who kept going and going.

"Hey, Maddie," I said, thoughtfully scratching my chin. "Don't we have a little revenge to wreak?"

Maddie giggled maliciously and nodded toward Jörgen. "You mean that pile of ooze over there, the one that sprayed us with icy water from the high-pressure washer?"

"He kind of looks like an easy target today," I said, meaningfully rubbing my hands together.

"It'll be like taking candy from a baby!" Maddie's smile was full of vindictiveness and conspiracy.

Like two female action heroes we sneaked off for the hose and turned the cold water on. To make sure that our revenge was served as cold as possible, we let the sun-warmed water in the hose run out, leaving in its place the really icy fresh-from-the-well water.

Jörgen seemed to be asleep under his cap when we turned the nozzle on at full power and let an ice-cold barrage of water hit his upper body. The water knocked his cap off and we could see Jörgen's utterly surprised face grimacing as the cold wet stuff whipped his skin. At first, the shock seemed to have made him completely powerless – he was sitting paralyzed with arms straight out, gasping for breath like a fish out of water. Then, suddenly, like an alarm clock on a Monday morning, the noise erupted.

"Aaaaaaarrrgh!" Jörgen waved his arms and screamed at the same time, and his chair tipped over backwards. It wasn't until he was floundering helplessly like a turtle on its back that we turned the water off.

The noise had scared Vibeke, who came running out, thinking that Jörgen had hit his foot with an axe or something. When she saw her husband lying on the ground, kicking and screaming in a big puddle of water, she burst out laughing.

Jörgen stayed on his back and blinked the water from his eyes. He rubbed his forehead and close-cropped hair a few times with his calloused fist before he finally sat up and looked around in confusion. It wasn't until he saw Maddie and me, folded over with laughter and still carrying the evidence in our hands, that he understood what had really happened.

"Why, you little …"

That was all we heard before we ran into the stable for cover. We could hear Vibeke's cheerful comments and laughter as Jörgen, muttering angrily, splashed toward the house to get out of his soaked clothes. Our revenge had been a total success!

Naturally, our spirits were high as we walked around in eighths on the riding course, warming our horses up before jumping. Vibeke had promised to come out and coach us while Jörgen "took a nap" with Isa. We still giggled now and then about our watery coup. Coolie felt alert and walked with elasticity in her bounding strides.

Once in a while she shot her head up to watch a gull on the field or a fluttering piece of plastic on a hay bale. Maddie had driven Shotster at a trot and was riding easily with half-long reins. Vibeke entered the riding court and started moving poles to prepare our jumping practice.

"I though we might try a little seat and balance work today," Vibeke said as she expertly adjusted the rails of an oxer.

"Prepare for muscle pains," I called out to Maddie and laughed. Vibeke worked us hard in her practice sessions, and we knew that when we slid off from our horses in an hour, our legs would be trembling like jelly.

"You can start trotting at the bars and land in a gallop by the first obstacle. Try to keep the horses long and low now, while we're warming up."

This last wasn't easily done with Coolie – she was drawn toward the first obstacle like a giant lump of iron to an enormous magnet. I had to shorten my reins a lot to hold her back.

"Ride her till she's obedient, Anna. Ride for the poles but turn just before, or stop and turn on the forehand." I could already feel a drop of sweat running down my neck and tickling me between my shoulder blades.

"Keep your chin up, Maddie. The horse will keep track of the bars and you aim for the next obstacle!"

There was a film of dust in the air behind us, and sweat

dripped as we struggled on the riding course. We counted gallop leaps and jumped without stirrups and with arms stretched outward. Vibeke certainly gave us the whole treatment. Coolie snorted with nostrils wide open, and my reins made white and lathery lines on her neck.

When the obstacles were raised, Vibeke told us how to sit.

"Relax your wrist, Anna. Keep your elbows parallel to your body. Right, that's good, Anna!"

I struggled with all the details, repeating a mantra in my head, "Elbows in, chin up, immovable legs!" Maddie's face was fiery red as she landed after the last obstacle of a three-jump combination. Maddie's greatest strength was dressage, and she had her hands full remembering the stride into the obstacle, helping her horse over it, and setting the correct course for the next obstacle. Shotster jumped well, considering that he was actually a trotter, and Maddie was a complete natural when it came to riding, so they learned fast. I realized that I could think such thoughts without feeling that old familiar tinge of jealousy that had always reared its ugly head whenever I met somebody who was really good. I'd managed to get over that feeling with Maddie, and was just glad and inspired that she was so good. Maybe it was because she was so humble and generous with praise for others that I sort of felt inoculated against any jealousy.

Maddie and I had really become good friends, and I found myself thinking less and less about my old best friend Linda. My old home town of Uppsala felt far away, and I always felt guilty that I forgot to call or e-mail Dad as often as I should.

"Okay girls, good work! That'll do for today. Take the horses for a twenty-minute walk to let them wind down. Ice-cream when you get back!" Vibeke said, giving us a thumbs-up. I wiped my face with my T-shirt and let my feet hang loose from the stirrups.

"I'm totally beat," I exclaimed, lying back in the saddle and resting on Coolie's broad hindquarters. I bounced until my riding helmet came down over my eyes.

"Vibeke's great!" Maddie said, nodding.

"Totally great!"

There was a calm over the countryside – a midsummer calm. The farmers seemed to have taken a day off for once. The silence was broken only by twittering birds, not by roaring tractors. I enjoyed thinking about having the house to myself and having a break from my terrorizing brothers. The summer was still ahead of us, even if a few killjoys kept telling us that, "from now on, it's going to get darker every day." I had hordes of fluttering happiness butterflies in my stomach, thanks to the realization that I was walking a crunchy gravel road on my very own horse. The cantle cut into the small of my back and I straightened up in the saddle. We silently walked our horses, rocking in the saddles and absently scratching their withers. I inhaled the sweet summer smells. Coolie clattered on under me, big and safe.

When the stable work was done and the horses taken care of, we padded home to my house and dedicated the rest of the day to just relaxing, eating, surfing the net and cuddling with Konrad, who totally enjoyed not having to share our attention with two crazy Irish setters.

I was awakened early Sunday morning by Konrad, who was washing my ears. It tickled so much that I screamed loudly. Maddie sat up in bed and blinked in confusion.

"What's happening? What is it?"

"Tongue in ear!" I explained, rubbing my right ear to get rid of the feeling of the rough cat tongue.

Maddie laughed, shook her head and said, "I thought we were being attacked and robbed – at least!"

After breakfast, we went to the stable. The morning chores were handled quickly by our practiced hands, and everybody knew what to do. Before lunch all the boxes were mucked out and the horses checked, fed and sprayed with fly repellant. The farrier was coming after lunch, and the horses that were getting a pedicure, as Vibeke liked to jokingly call it, had to stay inside. Spotlight angrily banged at his box door. He tried to inform us that he wanted to go out and eat juicy green grass right now, not stand inside a dusty stable, looking at nothing!

"How about a nice long ride?" I let the plastic curry comb slide through Coolie's well-brushed tail. "We can make it before the farrier comes, otherwise Coolie's feet will ache for two days and I won't be able to ride her!"

"Yeah, I think Shotster has some muscle pains since yesterday."

I suggested that we take the "lake road." It actually didn't go around a lake; just a big pond. It would take almost an hour and a half to get around it, which would be just about right.

"Oh, the 'lake road'? You mean that one that passes Birch Farm, where a certain Christian works?" Maddie treated me to a hilariously exaggerated wink.

"Oh, get out of here, you rat! It's actually just long enough, and it's been weeks since we rode there." I could hear myself sounding defensive and I could tell my cheeks were getting hot. Maddie just laughed and sang Whitney Houston's "I Will Always Love You" until the windowpanes almost shattered.

Of course, I'd never admit to Maddie, or to anybody else, that when I glimpsed the roof of Birch Farm a few nervous butterflies fluttered in my belly. I knew that he'd be working today, because we had talked about it at the dance, but maybe he was at lunch or something. Besides, what would I do if I saw him? Yell out, "Hey Christian, you're the most fabulous guy I know?"

I sat up as straight as I could, but in spite of Coolie's imposing stature I couldn't peek above the well-tended lilac hedge that surrounded Birch Farm. Then I heard the sound of somebody playing tennis. They shouted and yelled at each other and laughed between volleys. I listened to the sound of the ball being hit and harsh teenage voices. A strange feeling of déjà vu filled me – why were these voices so familiar, and why did I suddenly feel so uneasy? The disk drive that is my brain kept rattling, informing me that thought activity was in progress. Tennis balls …

"Maddie! These are the boys I heard!" I reined Coolie in and whispered desperately to Maddie, who walked Shotster up to me. Shotster couldn't always keep up with my long-legged Coolie.

"What is it, why are you whispering?" Maddie reined in Shotster, who was now elegantly parked next to Coolie.

"It's the boys I heard when I fell off; you know, the tennis ball and all that. I recognize that laugh and I know I heard it at the Månssons' the night that Sis ran away."

Maddie wrinkled her nose and looked as if she were repeating everything I had said at a slower tempo. Then her nose smoothed and she opened her dark-brown eyes wide at me.

"You mean these guys are the night riders?"

"They have to be! Everything fits."

"We have to talk to Christian! Come on!" Maddie purposefully turned Shotster around, like a hero in a Western movie, and aimed for the gate. There was some kind of doorbell with a microphone and speaker. Maddie quickly slid off her horse and pressed one of the buttons. After a few moments, there was a scraping sound in the box.

"Birch Farm, this is Gunilla."

Maddie explained that she wanted to see Christian, and Gunilla promised to tell him that we were at the gate. I stayed on Coolie's back – my heart hammered in my chest and my mouth was as dry as sandpaper. Birch Farm was surrounded by high fences and big hedges that made it impossible to see in. I could hear voices but didn't see anything. After a couple of minutes, Christian came sauntering over in dark blue work pants and a light green T-shirt with the Birch Farm logo.

"Hey, this isn't bad, two girls are after me! What can I do for you?"

As usual, he was so shamelessly tanned, and his hair was sun-bleached against his tan. I just wanted to ogle him, but instead I started checking my leathers and pretending to straighten Coolie's mane. It was a good thing that Maddie was there – she had common sense and she certainly didn't seem to be dazzled Christian's cute face and dazzling smile. She went up close to him, as if

82

she was worried that somebody would eavesdrop, and told him about our suspicions. Christian looked up at me, a troubled wrinkle between his eyebrows.

"Anna, are you totally sure these were the same voices?" At first I couldn't help thinking about how lovely it was to hear him say Anna, but then I thought that I'd better shape up and realize that this was actually a serious matter.

"They are the same voices; I'm a hundred percent sure. I heard them at Vibeke's and at the Månssons' farm."

Christian raked his fingers through his hair. He looked thoughtful.

"If I confront the boys they won't admit anything. These boys are pretty shrewd, and they've been around."

"But can they go out anytime they want?" I asked.

"No, not without being accompanied by the staff. This is pretty weird. If you know the dates when all this happened, I'll check our records to see who was working and what the guys were doing on those days. Maddie, you have my number, don't you? Can you phone me or text me with the dates when you get home?"

"No problem! Come on, Anna, let's go home right away." Maddie vaulted into the saddle and Christian held up his right hand to say goodbye, patted Shotster's hindquarters and then disappeared behind the gate again.

Maddie and I babbled excitedly about our new discovery in the night riders mystery. Just imagine if we caught them; it felt as we were in a thrilling mystery show or something. We fantasized about being interviewed by the press afterwards and becoming great heroes of the horse owners. For my part, I had some other fantasies too, of a more romantic kind, but I didn't have to tell anybody about those.

The farrier's van was parked on the yard and he was in the middle of taking care of Spotlight's hooves, with some difficulty. Maddie and I hurried to get our saddles off and put Shotster and Coolie back into the paddock again before excusing ourselves and almost running back to my house. I found my calendar and noted the dates when Amaryllis was hit by the tennis ball and when I was out looking for Sis. We also checked the forums where people had written about what had happened. A stable with Icelandic horses a couple of miles from Birch Farm had had visitors, and a small trotting stable had had somebody chasing their horses around in a paddock. Those horses also had marks on their bodies, as if they had been whipped. We noted the dates and texted Christian.

During the rest of the day we could hardly sit still while we waited for Christian to get back to us. We cleaned up after the farrier and prepared for the evening feeding before we called it a day at Vibeke's stable. Maddie decided to sleep over again and we made chocolate cake to pass the time. Just as we were cramming down the cake there was a knock at the door, and I jumped so violently that I dropped a piece on the sofa.

"Drat, I'm so used to the dogs being here, they always warn if somebody's coming to the door!" I explained, trying to clean the chocolate stain off the sofa. With two kid brothers, dogs and a cat, it was a good thing that the sofa cover was detachable and washable. Maddie jumped up and opened the door.

"Mm, smells good in here!" It was Christian, who, without hesitating, kicked his sneakers off and sniffed his way to the cake.

"Please, help yourself to a piece so we don't eat it all!" Maddie took out a plate and spoon. Christian looked happy and cut himself a big piece.

"I think I've worked out who they are, and this actually has some relation to chocolate cake." Christian settled down in a chair and started gobbling cake.

"What, chocolate cake? What do you mean?" Maddie leaned in and eagerly nudged Christian's arm as if she thought his explanation was too slow.

"You see, the boys have different nights when they're supposed to make some kind of dessert for the dining room, and they also have to clean the kitchen. All the dates fit in with the evening shifts of two certain boys. They must have wormed their way out the kitchen window and gone AWOL."

...?" I asked.

...old army draftee term, from my dad's day.
...go on a leave without telling anybody, if you
...at I mean. It means Absent Without Leave."
...ian smiled at me and I studied the rest of the
...olate cake on my plate and hoped that my face
...asn't as red as a fire hydrant.

"So what do we do now? Are we going to call the
police?" Maddie sounded excited.

"The police can't do anything; we have no proof and
they're short on manpower, so I doubt they'll put tails on
two teenagers who might go night riding." Christian scraped
off the last chocolate on his plate and licked his fingers.

"I think we'll have to go on a stakeout ourselves,"
Christian said, looking at Maddie and me with a little
sly smile.

"A stakeout? What do you mean, are we going to play
detective in the middle of the boondocks?" The thought
made me laugh.

"Yep, but you don't have to if you're scared,"
Christian said in an almost fatherly tone of voice.

"I'm not scared! If I can help keep all the horses safe,
including Coolie, I'll be a secret agent anytime!" The
firmness of my voice surprised me, and both Christian
and Maddie burst out laughing.

Chapter 7

Operation Catch the Nightriders was in full swing. We planned and intrigued like some super secret agents on TV. We decided not to tell anybody else about our plans, which wasn't that easy, not to me anyway. I almost spilled the beans to both Vibeke and Mom a couple of times. Christian had informed us that the two suspects were both on kitchen duty Thursday night, and he guessed that they'd make their getaway when the night staff came in, since that crew was smaller than the day staff, and that they'd make sure to get back before the night staff made their first round at one in the morning.

I was all mixed up with feelings of delight and fear, which both kept the adrenaline pumping. I guess we were pretty absent-minded in our work at the stable, and not even Coolie got the attention that she was accustomed to. The thought of Christian now gave me a thrill for more than one reason.

When Thursday night finally came, Maddie and I prepared for our mission. We chatted nervously as we chose clothes in dark, drab colors and pulled dark caps on our heads.

"Do you think we should smear our faces with mud, too?" Maddie suggested. I couldn't decide if she was serious or not, and we both laughed nervously. Mom raised a surprised brow when we said that we were going out biking, but we explained how important it was to be fit when you were riding and that there were camps and competitions coming up so we had to get in shape. She sighed and mumbled something about crazy horse girls.

We biked over to the place where we were going to meet Christian. Somehow, I had been looking forward to spending the evening next to Christian, hidden behind a bush, but to my disappointment his plan was quite different.

"You can hide here in the bushes. Text me if you see anything. I'll watch from the other side in case they go that way. Don't forget to turn off the your phone's ringtone!"

We obediently dragged our bikes into the bushes and carefully hid them. Maddie, ever practical, had brought two blankets in her handlebar basket, so that we could make comfortable beds on the grass. Soon we were lying with hearts pounding, staring up the little gravel road. Would we be able to catch the night riders?

We fought a no-win battle with the mosquitoes, which tried their best to empty our bodies of blood. Maddie shushed me when I slapped them too loudly. Sometimes the mini-vampires had company from ants, which seemed to be interested in climbing humans, so I made even more noise.

"Ssssh, there's somebody coming!" Maddie hissed, and I froze as if I had been petrified by a magic spell. My pulse raced. It was past eleven and twilight, but not dark, which is typical for Sweden this time of year. Steps crunched closer out on the road. I peeked out between blades of grass. The sound came closer and closer. Suddenly, I heard mysterious, almost panting breaths coming closer. I was paralyzed by fear and held Maddie's hand in a convulsive grip. Then the summer night silence was broken by a loud roar and something big and black threw itself at us. I buried my face in the blanket and heard myself screaming, a real horror movie scream.

"Rambo, come here! What are you doing, Rambo?" I heard a male voice bellowing somewhere. And suddenly a man in as sweatsuit entered the shrubbery, holding a big, black mongrel dog on a rope that acted as a leash.

The dog barked wildly at us, but finally the man managed to silence it before he scrutinized us up and down.

"What in all the world are you doing here, ladies? Lying in the bushes in the middle of the night?"

I frantically tried to find some kind of logical explanation without having to tell the truth about why we were lying there.

"We're watching birds," I surprised myself by saying, which made Maddie bury her face in the blanket and laugh hysterically.

"'Watching birds'? What would you see from in there? And you don't even have any binoculars." The man looked at us suspiciously and I realized that he actually had a right to think that we were the ones who were preparing something criminal.

"I have binoculars on my phone," I retorted, holding it up. The man looked suspiciously at my phone and then at Maddie, who was starting a new hysterical laughing fit.

"Well, I actually think you young ladies had better go home," the man said firmly. "Or else I'll call the police."

He strode off with his dog, which straggled and wanted to stay and sniff the two weird humans.

"Totally wonderful! 'Watching birds,' how did you come up with that?" Maddie sat up, wiping tears from her face with her sleeve.

"We have to leave. What if he calls the police?" I

crawled out on all fours and squinted after the man with the dog. He had walked some distance away from us but turned and looked back, which made me throw myself backwards and land hard on Maddie.

"Ouch, what are you doing?" Maddie rubbed her forehead, where my elbow had thudded into her.

"What if he comes back? I'm sorry, did I hurt you?" I patted Maddie's forehead as if that would ease the pain, but she moaned even more.

"Oooww, and then you hit me too, you nutso! Listen, birdwatcher, there's something called right of access to open country, and he can call the police as much as he wants to. We can take the opportunity to report his vicious dog that attacked us. Now sit down and be quiet, and try to remember why we're here!"

I was beginning to have second thoughts about how wonderfully smart our secret agent plan really was. I didn't appreciate being chased off by either mad dogs or cranky old men, or being eaten alive by insects, for that matter. Maddie, as always, was calmness personified and took out some cough drops, which we started eating. Then we looked through each other's cell phone photos. I had a cool close-up of Coolie raising her upper lip and baring her teeth – it was hopelessly funny. I forgot our mission and lay there giggling over our photos.

"Oops, a text from Christian!" Maddie pressed keys until the message was on her display.

"The night rounds are completed. Nothing more will happen tonight, so let's get out of here. I'll get back to you tomorrow. C."

We took our bikes from their hiding place and pedaled away in the darkness. As a preventive measure, I'd texted Mom that we'd met a few friends from the riding school and were talking to them. I had this strong feeling that Mom might not really appreciate that we were lying in the bushes outside a reformatory, watching for night riders, so I thought a little white lie was in order.

We had to wait five days for the next opportunity to catch the criminals, which was OK because I had lots to do – Maddie was at home, helping out with the trotters, while I took care of Vibeke's stable. It was time to repaint walls and boxes, and between painting sessions I sweated profusely as I took the horses out riding. My red neck got redder and was now decorated with colorful splashes of paint.

It was great to work full-time in the stable without being bothered by school and homework, but it was also a lot harder and more strenuous than one might imagine. I got calluses on my hands and wiry muscles in my arms from all the hard labor and heavy lifting. We finally took a day off from riding, and to my great surprise it was actually nice. It was one thing to take care of Coolie, but now I was riding two or three more horses every day. Mom laughed as I heaped giant servings of food on my plate, and told me that I ate like two lumberjacks.

When it was finally time to meet Christian again it felt almost like a well-rehearsed play. We set the sound on our cell phones to the off position and prepared our little hiding place almost like last time, but we had actually come up with a couple of improvements, like a bottle of bug repellant and better snacks.

"Well, I just hope that the geezer with the angry dog isn't out for a walk tonight," I said, grabbing a few cookies from the box.

"You can always pull the one about having binoculars in your phone," Maddie laughed, giving me a teasing shove with her elbow.

Maddie and I lay in our hiding spot chatting about riding, upcoming competitions and, of course, the riding camp that we'd signed up for. We had quite a few exciting projects ahead of us, and I was longing for and fearing them at the same time. Just as we were talking our way through our possible competitors in the ring, we heard feet crunching on the gravel. We immediately fell silent and squinted out through the branches. Before I saw anything, I could smell cigarette smoke. The people causing this air pollution were two boys who were sauntering along the gravel road. They wore baggy jeans and hooded sweatshirts with the hoods over their heads. They spoke softly and we couldn't hear what they were saying. Maddie texted Christian, telling him what was happening. As we saw the two shadows disappear around the corner of a green-painted barn, we sneaked out from our hiding place and Christian came jogging toward us. My heart made one of those silly little extra jumps that's usually accompanied by my cheeks turning embarrassingly red.

"Okay, let's follow them at a safe distance. Hopefully, their MP3 players are on so they won't hear us. Are you ready, my little special agents?" Christian blinked at us and I felt totally silly on my pink bike with a carton of cookies in the white handlebar basket.

"Oh, cookies! Anna, if you're a real cookie monster, how can you be that thin?" Christian laughed and grabbed a big handful of cookies from our carton. I felt totally confused; was that a compliment or did he think I looked like a bag of bones?

"Well, you're going to get fat soon anyway, the way you chomp those down!" Maddie retorted.

"Look, they're heading for Tina Persson's farm!" I pointed at two shadows turning onto the gravel road up to the farm. I knew that there were a few ponies out on their paddock.

"Let's take a shortcut across this field, and then we

can sneak up on them without them seeing us." Christina jumped the ditch and Maddie and I quickly laid our bikes down at the edge of the field and followed him. We crouched and ran as silently as we could through the low grass, toward a barn which we could hide behind but still have a view of the horses' paddock.

"Come on now, man! You're such a chicken," a hoarse voice said.

"A hundred if I do it?"

"Yeah, didn't I tell you? Don't lose your nerve now; we did it last time. These big, ugly oat eaters do what we tell them, you know!"

I hardly dared to breathe, but at the same time I was so angry that I could have dashed out and jumped those two guys. I thought that they'd hear both my heartbeats and my breath. Christian put an arm around my shoulder and pressed against me to get to the corner of the barn. His cell phone was out and he started filming. I could smell his deodorant as I stood pressed against him with his arm around me. I saw the thin gold chain he was wearing, looped around his tanned neck. I felt small puffs of his breath on my forehead. For a couple of seconds, I totally forgot why we were there and started dreaming about how Christian and I …

"Come on, you old horse-burger!" a harsh voice hissed. I heard the rustling sound of horses' hooves stepping in high grass. My little romantic moment was blown away and anger took over again. I thought about what they'd done to Vibeke's horses and what they might have done to Coolie.

"Come on!" Christian backed in behind the barn and waved us closer to him.

"Let's get out of here and call the police, and if they don't get here in time we still have my film as evidence."

"Aren't we going to stop them?" I was so agitated that my voice almost broke.

"That could only make things worse. I know these guys, and I don't want you to risk anything. The police can take care of this from now on." Christian put a protective arm around my shoulders and my knees suddenly turned to jelly.

"Now pedal home, and I'll wait here till the police arrive." He hugged me a little with one arm before letting go of me and dialing the police on his phone.

"Come on, Anna, let's go before they see us!" Maddie pulled at my arm and we ran back to the ditch where our bikes were parked. My body was full of a strange mixture of feelings that left me totally confused …

Chapter 8

The news spread like a California forest fire. Everybody was talking about the horse tormentors that had been caught and how we had pursued and trapped them. The rumors going around didn't always correspond to reality, and the rumormongers were making everything seem a lot more dramatic and dangerous than it had really been. One of them was about the night riders being on drugs and Christian knocking them down. Maddie's and my cell phones were now ringing all the time and suddenly everybody wanted to be friends with us and hear what had really happened. Mom, of course, went totally out of her head and gave me a long lecture about all the horrible things that might have happened to a sixteen-year-old girl. We got to sit down with the police and tell them over and over again what we had seen and how everything had happened. The criminals were moved to some other place, somewhere up the country, and we all sighed with relief.

Another interesting effect of our little secret agent adventure was that I now had Christian's number in my phone and that he texted me every now and then. No declarations of love, or anything, but still …

For a horse minder there's no time to bask in the glory and fame. I had lots to do. The stable was finally painted, which made me realize that the horses looked somewhat shabby. I took them all in, one by one, and went over manes and tails. The manes needed to be pulled and the tails cut. I groomed the docks of the ones that needed it and tended the fetlocks. I think there's a little professional groomer in me, because I just love to make horses look good and take care of them.

"You think you could do a little work on Jörgen later? His nose and ear hairs need some grooming," Vibeke said, teasing him. She was standing in the passageway, rolling the baby carriage back and forth to make little Isa fall asleep.

"Ewww – gross!" I laughed, making a disgusted face.

"That's just because I don't have any hair on my head – my hair has to sprout somewhere," Jörgen retorted, drawing his hand across his shaven head. He was putting up some new lamps.

I washed a scrape that Tartan had managed to get on his shinbone. He and Spotlight were like two rowdy little boys at summer camp, always covered with scrapes and wounds after their wild play in the paddock. I could never understand how they did it, because they frequently had wounds on their foreheads or on their croups. Tartan seemed to think it was relaxing to be groomed, now that they spent so much time in the paddock. He blinked a little with heavy eyelids and his lower lip trembled every once in a while. My fingers had sores after pulling all the manes, so I left Tartan's hairdo as it was, but I could groom his tail.

Vibeke and Jörgen disappeared into the house and I let Tartan out with his new, shiny look. I didn't groom Disa or her foal. I couldn't leave Mona alone in the paddock, and if she was inside there was no great chance that Disa would be left alone by her little two-month-old baby. So they stayed outside. Mona had just started running around and bucking in the paddock and took longer and longer turns away from her mother. I hung over the gate, enjoying the sight. Foals have to be some of the cutest things on earth! Her short, somewhat shaggy tail whirled like a helicopter in the air. She was so self-assured and cool, and moved as if she thought the world belonged to her. I dreamed about Coolie having a foal that would be all mine. That would be something!

And speaking of Coolie, it was her turn to be groomed now. Cissi, Tartan, Amaryllis and Spotlight had been through the process. My work day actually was over and I could do Coolie in my spare time. "Spare time" – well, that was the extra hours I spent in the stable after my official working day ended at three o'clock.

"Hi, my little butterscotch," I cooed as I pulled the halter over Coolie's head. She was kind enough to lower her head so I could reach up. I was so used to Coolie's imposing five-foot-one that all other horses seemed small to me. We sauntered up toward the stable and Coolie did her best to snap at juicy tufts of grass along the way. The dandelions shone like millions of small suns in the paddocks and cotton-wool clouds floated on a blue summer sky. I smiled at a tail-heavy bumblebee that fought gravity as it tried to land on a flower. What a wonderful summer; if it could just last forever!

Luckily, Coolie's mane had already been pulled, because of course I cared a little extra for my own horse. I groomed her carefully, washed and greased the gnat bites on her belly and shoulders and sprayed coat shine on her mane and tail.

"You're becoming so fine, girl!" I kissed her between the corner of her mouth and her nostril, that velvety groove that I found extra kissable.

I'd actually planned to go riding, but I was totally worn

out after the day's work so riding on my own just wasn't very tempting. I was embarrassed when I thought about how threatened I had felt when Vibeke told me that Maddie was going to help out in the stable. It felt like she was coming there to push me out to have Vibeke and all the horses to herself. Maddie was so good at everything and she'd made me feel like a silly little newbie, like those eager little girls at the riding school who jumped for joy if they were allowed to muck out a box or sweep the passageway. But now I missed Maddie when she wasn't here, and it felt lonely and a little dull to work in the stable without her.

At home, everything was back to normal, full speed ahead. Mom had picked up the kids at day-care – this was the last week before her vacation. I hoped that she and the twins would go somewhere so I could have the house to myself. It was most peaceful that way.

"Anna, you have to do your wash now. The laundry room gets totally full before you do yours."

I sighed deeply. Nag, nag, nag. I was hardly inside the door before she got going.

"Please, do you have to get on my case right away? I've worked all day and I'm really out of it."

"Have you ever thought about the fact that I work all day, every day, Anna? Not to mention driving and picking up the boys, shopping and cooking food. I really think you should start taking some responsibility now."

"Oh please, can't you stop nagging? I'll get to the wash before you have a stroke, okay?"

"Young lady, that attitude won't get you far …"

"Yeah, yeah, yeah, I know. I cost lots and lots of money and I don't do anything in the house and I'm just hopelessly expensive!" I interrupted her, walking into my room and banging the door shut so hard that the wall shook. Sis lowered her head and looked woefully at me.

"Oh, honey, it's not you I'm mad at." I lay down on the bed next to my chestnut red, silky-coated dog and buried my nose in her neck. My body ached from painting, my fingers stung from pulling manes, and the skin on my right forefinger was almost gone. I was so tired that I almost wanted to cry like a little kid, but Sis's calm breaths made me go to sleep instead. So there I stayed, at six in the evening, in grimy riding pants and a dirty sweater, snoring right through the night without even waking once.

The next morning, I sat up in bed, totally confused, wondering what day it was. Still groggy from sleep, I realized that it was the last Friday of June, a quarter past six in the morning. I sneaked up and let the dogs out without waking anybody else in the family. Konrad meowed his way to a bowl of milk and I made one of my own, with a mountain of Granola on top. Before going to the stable, I collected all my clean clothes and threw them on the bed in my room. Sorting and folding would come later.

The morning fog floated over the dew-damp fields in airy veils. In the haze, I could see outlines of grazing horses. I was too far away to make out who was who, but when I cupped both hands around my mouth and called for Coolie, one of the silhouettes raised its head and neighed in answer. I smiled happily to myself.

I started the day with the usual tour around the paddocks to make sure that all the horses were fine and check which of the paddocks needed more water. A few of the troughs needed cleaning before I filled them. I had my MP3 player going at full blast, so I jumped a couple of feet when I felt a hand on my shoulder.

"Oh, did I frighten you?" Vibeke was standing behind me, dressed in khaki shorts and a white top. Her hair had grown out so she could gather it in a little tuft on her neck. I took the earphones out of my ears.

"I was plugged in," I explained, holding up the earphones to show her.

"The corruption of youth; you'll all be deaf before you're twenty-five." Vibeke laughed, teasing me. "But I've got a little surprise for you," she went on. "I thought that you and I could go over to Stadstorp Farm today."

"Stadstorp? Isn't that Nina Linge's stable?"

"Right, and I thought we could take a couple of horses and let her see us ride." Vibeke looked expectantly at me.

"What, now? Who? We?"

"I knew that would surprise you! Won't that be fun? I have to get back to heavy training after my pregnancy if we're going to get out on the competition circuit again!"

I still hadn't really collected myself after the shock. Nina Linge was one of the best dressage riders in the country, with several World Cup victories to her name. I'd seen her on TV, elegantly riding her unbelievably beautiful stallion, Tango. First of all, it felt totally absurd that I'd even practice with Vibeke, who was an accomplished pro, but then also, we'd have an Olympic rider as our coach. How weird was that?

"But I can't ride for somebody like that!" I protested, feeling those nervous butterflies awaken in my belly.

"What do you mean, somebody like that? Nina's a real darling, and she coaches horses and riders in lots of different classes. I'm going there, anyway, to check out a three-year-old that she has for sale, so I thought we might take the opportunity to ride for her. Nina thought it would be fun, and I haven't seen her since Falsterbo last year."

"I can't go like this!" I declared, looking down at my very unwashed riding pants and my washed out T-shirt. As if clothes were my biggest worry. I'd probably look like an old bale of hay next to Vibeke. But on the other hand, I could at least try to be a clean bale of hay.

"So change before we leave. Now let's get Tartan and Coolie inside."

Suddenly, my relaxed morning in the stable had changed into nervous expectation and slight queasiness from stomach nerves. What would Nina think of Coolie? Maybe she would laugh and think that Coolie was a sway-backed, hopeless camel that you certainly couldn't ride for dressage. My thoughts floundered in my head and I wished that everything could just be normal, and that I would just ride here, at home, or in the riding ring with Vibeke as my teacher. But at the same time, there was something that drew me in and felt like a dream come true: just imagine going to Nina Linge's stable, meeting Nina and then actually getting to ride for her! I'd be an idiot to say no to that opportunity.

Coolie was groomed from top to toe. I greased her hooves and sprayed her mane and tail with coat polish. I brushed her until I couldn't find anything more to brush, and then I took out a newly washed sweat sheet, the new one I bought for Coolie. I carefully put her leg wraps on and laid her checkered sweat sheet over her.

"I'll run home and change!" I called to Vibeke, who was bending over Tartan's legs, fastening the leg wraps. If there were a world championship in leg wrap fastening,

Vibeke would certainly take a medal. She did four legs while I worked on one.

It took some time to choose the clothes I wanted to wear, but finally I went for a pair of dark blue, checkered riding pants, which happened to be the only clean pair I had, and a denim shirt with short sleeves. I brushed my hair and made a neat braid at the back of my neck.

A little later, sitting in the car with Coolie and Tartan in the transport, I felt a weird mixture of expectation, fear and joy, all at the same time.

"Won't this be great fun! It'll be a good preparation for the riding camp and the summer competitions for you and Coolie, don't you think?"

"Yes, of course, but how weird is it that somebody like me is going to be coached by Nina Linge?"

"Don't be silly, Anna! Don't think like that; try to realize that this is how you grow and become a better rider. You have to challenge yourself to get better!"

I sighed and nervously bit off dry pieces of cuticle. One of my cuticles started bleeding. I sucked on my hurt little finger and tried to mentally prepare myself for something that would be fun, good and instructive.

"Think about how jealous everybody will be!" Vibeke smiled, as if she had been reading my mind. And this was actually true – I especially wished that Camilla would hear that I had ridden for Nina. Camilla, who was a competition rider from the area, was the unparalleled queen of stuck-up and mean. Her dad bought horses worth hundreds of thousands of crowns (which is tens of thousands of dollars) for Camilla. We had been at the same jumping camp this Easter and she had laughed scornfully when I fell off Coolie. And then she had written mean things online about camels walking in Omset.

A little later, when we pulled into an alley surrounded by horse paddocks with very white fences, those darned butterflies started to do flips in my belly. Why had I said yes to this? Most probably, I'd just make a fool of myself and feel bad for months afterwards. Another little voice tried to persuade me that everything would work out fine, and that Nina would say that I showed great promise and that I could ride her horses in competitions. Yeah, right! Those butterflies kept flipping.

Nina's farm was well-tended but not as lavish as I would have expected. The main house was surrounded by lilac bushes and the stable was painted a pleasant red and had a heavy stone foundation. A few cats were lying here and there, enjoying the morning sun. When we opened the car doors, we were attacked by two cheerful Labradors. One of them kept sticking his muzzle in my crotch and I whirled around in embarrassment, trying to avoid his attention. It was while I was doing this awkward dance that Nina came walking toward us. I could feel my face going red.

"Bear, Gordon, into the stable!" Nina roared, and the two black Labs reluctantly sauntered into the stable, turned in the doorway and lay there, staring at us ruefully.

"Hi, Vibs!" Nina said, hugging Vibeke for a long time. "Didn't you bring your little wonder?"

"She's at home with Jörgen, so I can concentrate on horses for once! This is Anna, my horse minder."

"Hi, Anna. Welcome."

"Hi," I said with a thin, hollow-sounding voice. This always happens when I get nervous – I sound like the greatest nerd on Earth.

Nina seemed more down-to-earth than I'd expected. She was dressed in dark brown shorts, a worn T-shirt and a not completely clean beige-checkered riding vest. Her face was tanned and without makeup, her hair carelessly tied in a ponytail, and she had a beige cap on her head. On her feet, she wore a pair of very ugly slippers in an extremely loud cherry color. She was very different from the neat competition rider I'd seen in horse magazines, wearing tails, a top hat and a well-made-up face.

"You go ahead and unload; you can use the two boxes directly to the right. I'll put the kettle on." Nina fired a big smile at us before she walked toward the main house.

Vibeke and I unloaded the horses. Tartan ran down the ramp with a few funny jumps while Coolie slowly and calmly backed down. It was always great to load and unload Coolie – she really was totally cool.

Right after we'd unfastened all the protections, Nina came out carrying a tray with coffee and cookies. We sat down on the white garden furniture outside the stable.

"You want coffee or soda, Hannah?"

"Anna. Soda, please," I said, feeling a little hurt that she didn't even remember my name.

"Anna, of course! Typical me, I'm just rotten at remembering names. Sometimes I almost forget my own kids' names," Nina laughed, handing me a cola. Nina and Vibeke started talking about horses and horse people and I sat there totally fascinated, just soaking in every detail. They knew so much about everything that sometimes I hardly understood. What the heck is a "cadence"? I felt ignorant and stupid next to these old dressage pros.

"So, you want to start out by looking at the three-year-old?" Nina asked at last, when they had finished their coffee and I had eaten five cookies with soft chocolate nougat filling.

"Sure, how exciting!" Vibeke answered enthusiastically.

The three-year-old turned out to be a half-breed with distinguished bloodlines from Sweden and Germany. She was powerful but still noble, almost the same type as Amaryllis.

•

"Well, here's Elba!" Nina led the golden brown mare out on the riding track. The horse was bridled and saddled, but Nina started by lunging her while Vibeke and I sat on a wooden bench by the riding track.

"She's just beautiful!" I exclaimed as I saw Elba walking around Nina with springy steps. Elba's head nodded energetically in time with her walk. Her coat shone in golden nuances and lithe muscles played under it. I followed her with my eyes – Elba really was beautiful.

"What a lovely high step she has; a good walk is the foundation of everything!" Vibeke nodded in satisfaction. She had taken out a video camera and was following the horse's every movement.

"I own one of her sisters who is quite promising. I don't think you'd be sorry!" Nina looked satisfied when she urged Elba into a trot.

After a while, Vibeke mounted and tried riding her. I handled the camera, after having been carefully instructed about where the record and stop buttons were. Elba's training had just started and you could see that she was inexperienced. Vibeke had to use exaggerated aids and sometimes put her riding crop before and behind her leg to explain what she meant. She tried a few tempo changes and gallop strides. As usual, I enjoyed watching Vibeke in the saddle; she always made everything look so light, easy and harmonious.

"This is a lovely girl!" Vibeke said a little later, as she smoothly slid down from Elba's back.

"She's a real find, Vibeke!" Nina said, sending Vibeke a meaningful wink. "She might be your ticket to the Olympics!"

"Well, I guess that's the right kind of goal to aim for," Vibeke laughed. I stood next to Elba and let my hand slide along the graceful bridge of her nose. She had no white marks at all, but it looked as if somebody had blackened the lower parts of her legs and also her muzzle. Elba twitched her ears and sniffed for treats.

"It's tempting, and of course I'll think good and hard about it," Vibeke said, patting Elba's round hindquarters as Nina led the mare away.

Then the dreaded moment arrived. I sat on Coolie's back, about to be scrutinized by a star dressage rider. Just the thought made me giggle nervously and feel sick, all at the same time. What was I doing here? And on top of everything, Vibeke was standing on one long side and filming everything. I warmed Coolie up with some trotting and started breathing unnecessarily hard from that, probably forgetting to breathe properly because of my nervousness.

"Come across the middle line in serpentines, Anna. Start at a trot but slow down to a walk on the middle line and then go into a trot again."

111

I trotted into a serpentine and slowed on the middle line. Coolie felt a little gawky and stiff. I tried to bend her properly in the turns.

"Don't overbend her; it's all right if you can see her cheek. Straighten up that walk; you're staggering!"

I could feel sweat breaking out on my neck and temples. I fought with my big horse and tried to straighten and bend her by turns.

"Straight, straight, straight. That's it, good, Anna!" Nina's praise gave me new energy and I drove and shortened until my legs hurt. Coolie snorted and threw her head up in protest.

"Oh, I can see the lady is a little easy-going. Don't let her balk! Ride into the walk, drive! Drive, drive, drive!" Nina urged me on, clapping her hands to amplify what she meant. I drove and drove, my belly hurting.

"Watch that you don't lose her outside; keep it together! Her neck should be the highest point – don't let her hang in your hands!"

Her instructions battered me like a hailstorm. I fought like an animal and forgot both Vibeke's filming and Nina's World Cup medals. My mouth tasted like sand, dust and sweat, my body ached and the reins chafed my fingers. Only Coolie, Nina and I existed.

"Down into the saddle – if you get front-heavy she'll never get her hind legs under her. That's right, niiice!"

I fought with my outside leg and leaned back. Coolie's trot wasn't exactly soft traveling. After catching my breath by walking for a while I was relieved to gallop.

"Collect, drive, sit down, drive!"

I sat, I drove and I died ... almost. That was how it felt when finally, after forty-five minutes of drilling, I was allowed to walk a sweaty Coolie to calm her down. We had practiced galloping strides and tempo changes until both Coolie and I were totally soaked.

"That was nice, Anna. It looked really good at the end." Nina encouragingly patted my leg and also gave Coolie a well-earned pat. "As soon as you start riding with seat and leg you collect her quite nicely. If you want a horse this big to walk in form, you can't just sit down for the ride."

"I'm totally beat, and my legs are spaghetti – overcooked spaghetti!" I laughed when I carefully eased myself down on the ground.

"Good work, Anna! You really went for it, and I have the evidence right here!" Vibeke smiled as she held her camera up.

"So, now it's Tartan's turn," she went on, walking toward the stable.

I tied Coolie up in the water box and let tepid water run over her sweaty body. She snorted into the water and tried to swallow as much as she could. It looked so funny that I couldn't help laughing. I raked excess water away with a scraper, making swishing sounds, and Coolie's coat shone almost black. Soon, she was standing in the spacious extra box with her sweat blanket on and a big armful of juicy hay to chew. I took the opportunity to rinse my face in cold water before I went out to watch Vibeke riding.

They were in full swing when I came out and I sat down and just enjoyed it. Vibeke and Tartan were like one. My legs were still shaky, but I felt exhilarated and happy. Coolie and I had ridden for Nina Linge, and although we weren't the best in the world, or even in Omset, we had managed pretty well. When I was actually sitting up on my horse's back I'd worked so hard keeping track of outside reins and inner legs, shoulders and hind legs, that I had forgotten who I was riding for.

When Vibeke had ridden Tartan until his neck was white with lather, a horse-keeper came out with an exceptional horse. It took me a couple of seconds to see that it was Tango. A fully muscled stallion that does the highest levels of dressage is something truly unique. Tango had such stature and charisma that I almost got tears in my eyes.

"Have you ever ridden a World Cup winner before, Anna?" Vibeke called with an inviting gesture toward

114

I snuffled and tried to wipe the tears off my face with my sleeve.

"Poor girl, she can't even read. Horselover93." I slammed my laptop shut and threw myself face down on the bed. Why was it impossible to be happy? Something would always come up to destroy your happiness. I sobbed and sniffled; everything was just hopeless. How could I go to the riding camp after this? Camilla was sure to be there, and everybody else who had been taunting Coolie and me. Who had filmed the jumping camp? Suddenly, it felt like I was all alone in the world. Everybody just wanted to hurt me, hurt me, hurt me.

"Honey, what's wrong?" Mom had heard me crying and now sat down on the edge of the bed with her worried-mother face. This made me cry even harder and between sobs I managed to get out what had happened.

"What rotten girls did that? Are they supposed to be friends? Honey, it's going to be all right, I promise. In a while everybody will forget. People like that always get what's coming to them, so don't worry about them."

Usually, Mom's wisdom felt comforting, but today it mostly felt like she didn't understand at all. Nothing would make this better, and the whole summer was totally ruined!

"I don't know if I want to go to the camp."

Vibeke looked at me with her forehead wrinkled.

"Why? You and Maddie have been looking forward to this camp since spring. Of course you're going!"

"I thought I might ease up a little on riding for the rest of the summer. I'm sure I'll ride a lot when I go to the riding high school." I feverishly rubbed the bridle I was polishing and kept staring at it to avoid meeting Vibeke's eyes.

"But that only gives you more reason to stay in shape and to keep your horse in shape. Coolie is getting better and better right now."

Vibeke was sitting with little Isa in her arms. The baby had awoken just in time for our little leather cleaning session. I loved the smell of leather soap and enjoyed seeing the leather shine from leather conditioner. Normally, this was a nice little moment when Vibeke and I would sit chatting. This time, I was squirming like a worm, uncomfortable from being pressed and too embarrassed to tell Vibeke what had happened.

"Actually, I feel just a little oversaturated with riding right now and Coolie might need to take a rest for a month or so," I tried, feeling ashamed for being such a coward, a pitiful little sissy who ran and hid when the big kids were mean.

"Coolie hasn't been working for more than six months, she was resting almost all of last year, and anyway, she'll have a week off while you're staying with Maddie! Come on, Anna, what's the matter with you? It isn't like you to chicken out like this."

"Oh, I don't know. I just don't feel like it." I rubbed and rubbed the noseband while tears of shame burned under my eyelids. I swallowed hard and tried to keep from crying by conjugating verbs. Do, did, done. Go, went, gone. And so on.

"Hey, why don't you take a day off tomorrow? Go to the beach or just chill out with the dog at home." Vibeke put her hand on my back and moved it in small circles, as if she was trying to massage the evil away.

"But what about the horses?"

"I'll take care of the horses. You've been working hard, and you might need some time off. Sleep, eat and chill!"

Usually, it would feel like punishment not to go to the stable and take care of the horses, but weirdly, this time it almost felt like a relief.

I slept in on my day off. I had breakfast in front of the TV and let Mom and the twins go to the beach without me. Sis was beside herself with happiness, having her mistress home, and swaggered behind me wherever I went.

The sun was shining from a clear blue sky and I really should have gone out to enjoy the lovely summer weather but I didn't have the energy. I lay on the sofa, wearing the same T-shirt I'd been sleeping in, watching one worthless soap after the other. Reruns of Dr. Phil and Oprah came on in turns, and Oprah showed dogs that had been saved from a hurricane. The dogs were then reunited with their overjoyed owners – I cried rivers and had to get a roll of toilet paper to wipe my tears.

I refused to open my laptop, refused to go out and do something worthwhile. I lay there counting all the bad things that had happened, saving them up like small pearls of badness and threading them onto a necklace that I would wear. I felt sorry for myself and ashamed about how pathetic I was. A wonderful day off …

Mom and my brothers came home, sunburned and loud. Jonatan's and Kalle's hair was still wet. Their little bodies were golden brown and covered with scratches. They were overjoyed by the popsicles in the freezer. I wished I was four again, when a green popsicle could make everything wonderful.

Mom watched me with a little mischievous smile. I hoped she wasn't going to give me some cheerful pep talk right now.

"Have you had a nice day?" she asked. I was lying draped over the sofa, doughy and unclad, and the coffee table was covered with the leftovers of my provisions: empty cartons of crackers, a glass with deposits of orange juice, apple cores and candy wrappers. I was bewildered when she didn't mention the mess, or at least say, "Anna, are you really going to lie here when the weather is so nice outside?"

"So, have you been online today?" Mom said, and I could feel my annoyance crouching, getting ready to attack.

"Yeah, right. Of course I love seeing the entire world laughing at how worthless I am," I said with sharp irony. Mom stayed calm, still wearing her secretive smile.

"Well, I still think you ought to check out YouTube," she persisted, and my cheeks turned red with anger.

"Are you totally out of your mind? Can't you see this is hurting me?" I heard my voice turn to a scream, finally breaking from all the crying that wanted out. Mom sighed and put both her hands on my shoulders.

"Darling Anna, I understand that this has been rough. Vibeke called me. She's worried about you, too."

I drew a sharp breath. Vibeke? Was she mixed up with all this now? That was even more embarrassing!

"Now go to YouTube and search for 'Anna rides dressage.' Just do it, Anna!"

I sauntered into my room and turned my computer on. I really didn't understand a thing. After one or two eternities the computer finally found the Internet and I could load YouTube. I typed in "Anna rides dressage." To my great confusion, a film came up. My heart pounded when I pressed the play button.

It started with a piece of classical music, and then

123

Coolie and I came galloping. The music fit perfectly with the galloping rhythm and, unbelievably, I looked quite professional. My posture was straight and my hands worked nicely. I was shocked! I knew that galloping was Coolie's best gait, but I could never have dreamed that she could look that graceful and rhythmic. My lovely, beautiful Coolie!

After the galloping sequence, that was just a little more than a minute long, came the piaffe on Tango. The music changed to a pop song that fit perfectly with Tango's piaffing. I actually think that I've seen Nina ride a choice of rider presentation program to that song. As always, Tango was a wonder of shiny coat and rippling muscles. I was totally dumbstruck from wonder: I didn't see a clumsy oaf who couldn't ride – I looked good! Of course, anybody would look good on Tango, but I just felt so proud about the sequence with Coolie's collected gallop and, for the icing on the cake, Tango's and my advanced dressage move. The film ended with Nina applauding my show and doing thumbs up into the camera. I pressed play again, and again, and again.

"What do you think about that?" I heard Mom's voice behind my back.

"It's just too much! Who did this? Was it Vibeke? It's just too much!" I was jumping for joy. It was completely unbelievable that Vibeke had gone through all the trouble of editing the film and posting it on YouTube.

"Why don't you check out the comments," Mom said, giving my neck a loving little shake.

There were ten comments. I read them and my smile just grew. Nobody was mean, nobody called Coolie a camel. Most of them praised Tango for being so beautiful and I could only agree. But then, there were a couple that I kind of got stuck on and read over and over again:

"Capable girl and beautiful horses. Cellophane."

"Great to see this nice dressage. Who's the rider? Dressagedenise."

"Beautiful horses." That meant that Coolie also was included. My beautiful horse! I was so proud that I almost exploded.

"Feeling a little better now?" Mom asked, and I turned around and hugged her, the one single hug becoming longer and harder than all the hugs I've ever given her before, I think.

"It feels just great!" I laughed. "I think I'll go over to Vibeke's and ride a little in the woods on Coolie. She has to stay in shape for the camp and the summer competitions!" Mom winked at me and I rummaged in the wardrobe for a pair of riding pants.

Watch out, people. Anna is on her way!